JAY TINSIANO

Ghost Order

Please note: This book uses British English spelling and terms. Readers who are used to American English might notice a difference in the spelling or usage of some words. For example: tyres (instead of tires), boot (instead of trunk), and trainers (instead of sneakers).

All characters are entirely fictitious and not intended to portray any real person(s), dead or alive.

Acknowledgements

I would like to thank the following for their support and input with the production of Ghost Order.

Jay Newton
James Newton
Diane Velasquez
Dorene Johnson
Gavin Reese
Diane Geraldizo
Jane Davies
Vivien Holliday
Amber Morant
Tony Crewe
Saundra Wright
Lynn Hallbrooks
Jim Bronson
Eileen Mitchell
Melinda Jones
Ken Lingenfelter
Ann
Pete Bennett
Jan Simmons

Prologue

(AUC) Autodefensas Unidas de Colombia base camp

  Putumayo, Colombia

  June 1999

  Through the window, the rain cascaded down in continuous waves, battering the tin roof with its insistent drumming, pouring down onto the wooden steps.

  Outside, a group of soldiers in deep green fatigues moved across the camp and hurried inside one of the long huts that made up part of the barracks, slamming the door behind them. A small bedraggled dog, having made the camp its home, scavenged around a pile of rubbish piled up at the side of a smaller hut. Under the torrential rain, a sodden flag of the Autodefensas Unidas de Colombia – representing the new umbrella organisation that brought together a large number of right-wing paramilitary groups – hung lifelessly on a pole fixed to the barracks hut wall.

  To the agent present, it made no odds that this paramilitary group was connected to the cartels or the wealthy Colombian landowners or even that they were responsible for tens of thousands of deaths inside the country. He had a job to do; even if that meant aligning with the Devil. So be it.

  He had been fully briefed on the backgrounds of the leaders he was addressing now; how they had amassed their fortunes through emerald smuggling, kidnapping, arms dealing, robbery and, of course, the default source of income for many cartels; drug trafficking.

Yes, it was clear who he was dealing with. No one needed to remind him how precarious the tightrope of influence was over the muddy waters of South America and he knew he had to be careful how he handled the upcoming meeting.

He drained his coffee mug with one long pull, put it down and reached in his shirt pocket for yet another cigarette.

Through the window, the agent could see a black 4X4 pull up. Two men in AUC uniform jumped out and hurried across to the hut where the agent waited.

The two Colombian paramilitary leaders entered and shook hands with the agent, formally introducing themselves according to the expected military protocol, even though everyone in the room knew who each other was.

Gustavo Bejarano, the leader of the AUC, a tall, gruff-looking man with pockmarked cheeks shook the agent's hand. His subordinate, answering to the name Moreno, was a stout figure wearing mirrored sunglasses, which the agent would later figure out was a permanent fixture of his appearance no matter what the weather. Both men looked like gangsters in their ill-fitting uniforms. The agent also knew from his file that Bejarano had once been a member of the Medellin drugs cartel and had built a significant power base in Colombia off the back of it. The leader of the cartel, Pablo Escobar, lured two of Bejarano's allies to the self-built La Catedral prison, accused them of betrayal, then murdered them both with his own hands. Bejarano had also been summoned on that day but strongly suspected he was in danger and didn't go. After that incident, Bejarano allied himself with the rival Cali cartel against Escobar and from then on, the drug lord's days were numbered.

"We welcome you to our base of operations," grunted Bejarano, glancing down at the empty coffee mug on the table along with an open map.

"Well, I see you've had your coffee, so what have you got for us?"

The agent leaned over the map and pointed to a spot marked with a red cross. It was the identified location of a FARC camp (Revolutionary Armed Forces of Colombia or Fuerzas Armadas Revolucionarias de Colombia in Spanish), the Marxist-driven force that had plagued Colombia since the sixties.

"Our surveillance has identified this base where Commander Jiménez is in hiding – a mile over the Ecuadorian border across the Putumayo river. I'll take point on the mission but leave the tactics to your excellent team," he continued, deliberately stroking their egos. "However," he said, pausing for emphasis, "I insist on going in with the first wave. I'm sure you're well aware of the high possibility of detection by the FARC camp as well as from the Ecuadorian authorities, so I'd suggest finding a point to land the teams at least five klicks away and we make the rest of the way on foot. The terrain isn't ideal, but the cover is good enough."

"And what happens to Jiménez?" asked Bejarano, studying the agent closely with his beady eyes.

"As per our arrangement. We need an interrogation window to get what we want from him. After that, he's all yours," the agent replied, knowing full well that would be a green light for Jiménez's death.

Moreno turned towards him, a flicker of a smile forming.

"So you know. We don't fuck about down here. We will drain the sea to kill the fish, my friend."

The agent nodded as if in agreement, but was not entirely sure of his meaning.

***

At dawn, two squads of six men moved silently through the jungle as they formed a dragnet around the FARC camp. As planned, two choppers had carried in the soldiers, dropping them off in an open clearing on the far side of the muddy Putumayo River, just inside the Ecuadorian border.

The agent, armed with standard-issue AK47 and dressed in AUC fatigues, tucked in just behind the main advance. When the camp was under a kilometre away he split off with a three-man squad of Moreno's men in a pincer movement towards Jiménez's supposed location at the East side of the camp.

They crouched down within sight of their target location – a long Nissen hut draped in camouflage nets. Behind it lay another cluster of smaller huts, all with the same netting. In the fresh morning air they heard the snuffling of pigs from some unseen stall and through the gaps between the buildings they caught a glimpse of an antenna dish.

The agent was concerned.

Too quiet.

Where the hell was everybody?

They didn't have to wait long for the fireworks to begin. The first contact came within minutes. Crackling gunfire ripped apart the peaceful dawn, causing a chorus of animal screams and howls at their rude awakening. The small arms fire from the AUC gunman, west of the camp, increased in intensity.

The thump of explosive force ripped through the trees then a fireball engulfed one of the outside perimeter huts. That was the RPG team unleashing hell and their signal to move.

The squad leader, followed by the two privates, moved quickly to the target hut, weapons focused on the shuttered windows. There was a loud crack as a boot broke down the door and the soldiers stormed inside. The agent followed them in, his pistol in front of him.

The paramilitaries cleared each area inside the sparse accommodation that consisted of two bedrooms, a living area, toilet and a kitchen.

Empty.

No one home.

The agent in frustration kicked an empty crate that careered across the floor.

"Whatever was happening here is gone, we fucking well missed it," he hissed.

One of the soldiers glanced around casually, almost as if their enemy's disappearance was entirely expected.

"All right. Go join your commander," the agent said, reluctantly, before pulling open a bag of clothes that was lying on the floorboards.

The soldiers left just as a staccato of small arms fire resumed in the background. Commander Bejarano's men were clearing out the last remnants of resistance and searching the camp.

The agent continued searching but found nothing except the evidence of a quick escape; strewn clothing, a broken radio, a coffee pot with still-dirty mugs placed on top of a makeshift table made from boxes and a section of flat wood. He reluctantly gave up and headed to the middle section of the camp to find Moreno.

The AUC soldiers had rounded up a small group of FARC survivors; all young, both male and female dressed in civilian clothes. Another three AUC men were stripping off the dark olive uniforms from the dead bodies of FARC guerrillas, leaving their corpses strewn on the ground dressed only in their underwear, limbs flailing in the mud. The agent counted ten men and four young women among the dead.

Another soldier came with a jerry can found amongst the camp supplies and placed it on the ground. Moreno looked up.

"No sign of our friend?"

"No, they must have had lookouts by the river," the agent replied.

Moreno let out a low, guttural laugh. "Si, that is most likely. Your gringo technology doesn't work so well out in this country. Perhaps you should leave the insurgent hunting to us."

The agent ignored him and glanced around the now-quiet camp. There were cables tied to tree branches that led to the satellite dish he glimpsed earlier creating some early warning system for their communications. As smoke drifted lazily through the camp from the earlier explosion, he followed their line with his eyes and saw the cables led directly into the hut he had just searched.

Another FARC prisoner, a bit older than the others, stumbled into the central circle of prisoners, shoved by an AUC soldier who had found him. Moreno gestured impatiently to the soldier, who pushed him into a line with the other prisoners, then gestured at the gasoline.

The agent watched as the first male prisoner was doused in gasoline, the liquid running freely over his hair, face and exposed body. The man sobbed and begged, evidently realising what was happening.

"Where is Commander Jiménez?" Moreno demanded.

The man shook his head, refusing to open his eyes. "Please! Please! I do not know!"

This is interesting, the agent thought, taking out his cigarettes. A small part of him wanted to stop this apparent insanity, this drift into evil. The prisoners were all so young.

Yet it was also intriguing. Would these "hard" tactics produce the information needed? How many of them would Moreno burn to get what he wanted? These were unfortunate circumstances, and this was war, he reasoned. Even so, the agent steeled himself to watch.

Moreno asked again.

"Palma Roja, they went to Palma Roja!" the man blubbered between rapid gasps.

"Bullshit," Moreno countered. He wore an expression of boredom as he fished out a box of windproof matches from his pocket.

The agent saw the match strike in Moreno's hand, the flicker of flame drew all eyes toward it like bees to honey.

There was a pause, the silence thick with tension.

We will drain the sea, to kill the fish.

Then, with a casual flick of fingers, the match flew through the air. A small, fragile dancing flame – almost dying – just before the fuel on the prisoner ignited it back into life.

Chapter 1

County Cork, Ireland

Frank Bowen headed up the winding lane, cutting through endless fields until he came to a crossroads and stopped to consult the map. He knew it was around here somewhere, but the fact that it was hard to find was a good thing.

He changed up a gear and drove the rented Audi A3 straight across, towards the grey sky opening up ahead. Fast-moving clouds painted a stark backdrop behind a row of silhouetted trees. At a fork in the road that he recognised from the map, Frank drove onto a narrow lane and followed the twisting uphill road for several miles. He was soon passing old houses and farms, with their tumbling stone walls and towering corrugated hay sheds dotted here and there, and then came to an open five-bar gate partly obscured by a group of trees.

This must be it.

He drove along the track, mostly unused judging by the long grass sprouting from the occasional crack in the road, until a farmhouse came into view. As he pulled into the courtyard a spectacular vista of a lush green rolling valley with a dark blue sea sparkling in the distance came into view. A green Ford Explorer was already parked up on the gravel and a young man, who Frank guessed was the estate agent, was speaking into his mobile. He gave Frank a wave of his hand and finished his call.

Frank parked up, exited his rental car and nodded at the man.

"Mr Hales. How're ya doing? Grand day for it?" he responded cheerfully.

Any day, it seemed, was a good day when it wasn't raining in Ireland.

Frank gave an easy smile, almost forgetting he'd used an alias. "As long as it's dry, Mr O'Farrell." He turned to the main house, looking up at the roof as if surveying it. "So this is the Manor House?" he quipped.

The young estate agent nodded, following Frank's gaze. "Aye, it was a farm for many years. It's a great property but, as I said, has been on the market for a while. Let me show you around inside first, so."

They toured the farmhouse. It had a large central kitchen with wood-burning stove and an impressive dining room, as well as a front living room. Upstairs were four spacious bedrooms and an attic that spanned across the top of the building. The curtains were faded as were the carpets and the walls showed evidence of scuff marks and scrapes. The air inside was musty and beams of dust-laden sunlight streamed through the windows, adding to the sense of neglect and abandonment.

However, Frank warmed to it straight away. It felt like home. They then walked down to a dimly lit basement, divided into two rooms. The stone walls were covered with dark soot, old rusty farm gear was scattered on the concrete ground, and old wood shelves creaked with tins of paint and boxes of forgotten tools.

They walked back outside. "It comes with around two acres of pastureland, including the cow shed over there," the young agent gestured at the curved roof. "You could take it down, I guess." They walked to a stone building that had presumably been used for wood storage, but was now simply piled high with discarded furniture and rusting appliances, junk the previous owners had seemingly thrown inside from the house.

A small patch of woodland stretched from one side of the property for a few hundred yards with a stone wall cutting across. "That's part of the property boundary, up to the wall," the agent explained with a sweeping hand.

"How come no one's been interested?" Frank asked, turning to O'Farrell who made a face as if the answer personally puzzled him. "Just one of those properties that doesn't get sufficient interest, so. There were some offers but they just fell through."

Frank looked around again. It was a contender and, due to the lack of offers, it was highly likely he could negotiate hard on a price reduction. He would, however, need to carefully consider his dwindling finances and personal situation before making any commitment.

Chapter 2

CIA Headquarters, Langley

Brett Fallon, Head of Field Operations, tapped the screen, reading through the decrypted updates from one of his many HUMINT assets on the ground in South America. The continent had been his turf for a few years now, but he had taken over just as the significant action had wound down. The high-profile hunt for Pablo Escobar had ended with him being killed on a Medellín rooftop in 1993 after Fallon's section in the agency had become embroiled in an ongoing drugs war. Of course, the drug business hadn't ceased in the slightest. Other cartels had picked up the slack without a blip and Fallon certainly had his work cut out trying to stem the rising flood of drugs reaching the streets of American cities. However, as the media attention had shifted away from the drug war, budget allocations had been reduced even though the threat remained as high as ever.

His computer beeped. It was a reminder alarm for an urgent brief with the Deputy Executive Director, Kate Foster. He wondered what it was all about. Fallon himself reported directly to the Deputy Director for Operations, Greg Reinhart, a pay grade below Foster, so this was a rarity.

After another five minutes, he logged out of the terminal, shut everything down and headed off towards the East Wing, via the coffee station.

A shakeup, that's all it could be, he thought. The management and pen-pushers were moving personnel like chess pieces vying for some obscure organisational advantage and that – most likely – meant bad news for him and his current set-up.

He approached a ramped metal walkway that led to the SCIF (sensitive compartmented information facility) that kept listening electronic ears at bay in an encased "bubble", as it was nicknamed.

After swiping his pass key through the access portal, Fallon walked into the elongated meeting room where his superior and Foster stood talking at the far end in front of a large blank monitor screen affixed to the wall.

"Mr Fallon. Thanks for joining us," she said, gesturing to one of the chairs at the top of the table.

Fallon gave Reinhart a "what's going on?" look, which was ignored, and slipped into the chair. The superiors took their seats and Reinhart tapped a few keys on his laptop that booted the screen monitor into action, lighting up the blank screen with a Top Secret CIA emblem.

"Naturally, it goes without saying none of what we're discussing today leaves this room, Mr Fallon," said Foster.

"Naturally," Fallon replied.

Satisfied, Foster indicated to Reinhart to continue with a nod.

Reinhart pushed a file across the table to Fallon and gave him a moment to open it up.

"Some big changes are happening in the intelligence community," Foster began, fixing Fallon with her green eyes. "For some time we've been aware of the infrastructure being put into place for a new global agency: G13COMM. Reinhart will bring you up to speed." She turned to Reinhart, who clicked his mouse revealing a covertly taken photograph of a mousy looking man with reddish hair getting out of a car.

Reinhart cleared his throat. "This is Carl Paterson, head of a small, secretive set-up in Britain that started as an alliance between the British secret service and GCHQ while on the hunt for a whistleblower last year. The group is codenamed Ghost 13." Reinhart sipped his water, changing the slide to a photo of an older US military man with short white hair. "This is Colonel Dean Wexhall, originally attached to U.S. Army Special Operations. He is now detailed with running what is known as Operation Darkwood: the creation of a new agency – G13COMM – with intelligence and military capabilities that will swallow up the British operation, effectively merging them. Yes, Brett?"

Brett had leaned forward, opening his mouth to speak. "So Ghost 13 was originally a Brit creation and now it's set to expand under Wexhall?"

"Correct, except the agency is already up and running from what we understand," Foster clarified.

Brett nodded. He assumed they had an asset inside to have this up-to-date information.

"So, what is the mission for this new agency?"

"We don't know everything. There's a very tight lid on it, and this is pretty much all we can share with you at the moment."

Foster and Reinhart both fixed eyes on Fallon.

"You will need to hand over all your current operations to Lisa Graham and focus on uncovering as much detail on Darkwood and G13COMM as possible. I'm sure Graham will do an excellent job," said Foster.

"Wait a minute. I'm up to my eyes right now. I can't just abandon assets in the field—"

"You're not abandoning anyone," Reinhart interjected. "Graham has the skill set to take over your role."

Fallon shook his head. "She needs more time."

Reinhart and Foster exchanged glances.

"Then you will need to split roles. This is a priority. I'm sure I don't need to spell out that any rival intelligence group like G13COMM is going to be bleeding budget dollars away from us."

"You're saying the Agency is under threat from that tin-pot operation?" Fallon waved a hand at the screen, dismissively.

"That 'tin-pot operation' has some very powerful backers. We're not here to argue with you, Mr Fallon."

Fallon sighed. He was right. Someone was playing chess.

"Alright. What do you want me to do, exactly?"

Chapter 3

London

Below, the patched squares of green fields, snaking roads and dotted buildings spread far into the distance, fading on the horizon where the blue sky appeared. Sunlight glinted off the wing and Frank turned away to sip on his black coffee. The captain announced over the PA system that they were to be arriving at Heathrow airport in ten minutes and went through the usual monologue of resetting seats and tray tables.

Frank hardly heard any of it as his mind drifted back to how his life had changed in the last few months. The family he thought he was part of had been shattered when Maria asked for a separation.

Temporary, of course. See how it panned out.

It had knocked him off balance, shooting him between the eyes like so many of his adversaries had tried to do. Anger, hurt and betrayal all mixed into a cocktail of negative emotion had boiled up inside.

Then, after weeks of talking it through, he began to understand. The kidnapping of Joe and Maria must have percolated in her mind, giving her a different perspective of their relationship. The safety of their family was paramount to her and so she had dealt him the separation card. There was no way he could argue about being able to keep them safe in his line of work. Now he believed he was done with all that. There had been a few short-term contracts in security work. Nothing too dangerous but the damage, it seemed, was already done.

He loved her still. How could he not? She was the mother of their children. The one woman he would kill for and, indeed, had killed for.

Frank made his way through the lines at immigration, picked up his gym bag and made his way out into the harsh New Year's air to flag down a taxi. The cab driver gave him a nod at his instruction and Frank stared out from the rear window, still lost in thought, as they weaved through the hectic London traffic towards Stoke Newington. After thirty minutes he exited the taxi outside his small flat located above a twenty-four-hour convenience shop. People went about their business at all hours on this busy road. An Asian man unloaded boxes of vegetables onto the pavement. In his peripheral vision he caught a glimpse of a figure throwing a cigarette butt onto the road before moving off. Out of habit, Frank took note; middle-aged, tall and dark-haired, wearing a black leather jacket and faded jeans who was looking his way.

Was there something in it? Or was he being paranoid?

Frank bought cigarettes from the shop, then came back out and caught another glimpse of the same man turning the corner. He took his time fishing out his keys, managed one more glance and noticed the figure had disappeared.

Frank unlocked the door to the apartment, edged past the bicycles parked in the hallway and climbed the stairs. Once through his door, he looked around the sparsely furnished flat, checking each room for any sign of tampering.

Satisfied everything seemed in order, he grabbed a ready meal from the fridge, placed it in the microwave and grabbed a bottle of Jack Daniels bourbon and a glass from the cupboard before slumping onto the ageing sofa. The TV sparked into life and he tossed the remote aside, wondering how he had ended up back in the single life. He should be in Islington with Maria and the kids in the house that they had bought after moving from the flat in Shoreditch.

Now here he was, back in bachelor mode; alone in a cold, spartan flat.

Perhaps his idea of starting a new life in Ireland was too much of a stretch? It was barely affordable with his meagre savings and Maria hadn't worked since the kidnapping episode a year before.

Yet the farmhouse had felt perfect. Isolated but calm.

A family could live there under the radar. It could be a lovely card to play; an olive branch to offer her.

Who was he kidding? She wanted this. He wasn't to blame. Perhaps it was karma from when he left Jodie all those years ago. He had been young – what a naive idiot. The beep told him that his prepackaged meal was ready so he grabbed his Bolognese and wolfed it down.

Although he barely admitted it to himself, a deep part of him missed the adrenaline rush of being in the field, taking risks and holding the cold steel of a weapon in his hand. Instead, he had the prospect of an early morning shift, merely walking around a warehouse checking that everything was in order while his thoughts stewed and swirled.

Frank tossed the empty plate and cutlery in the sink to fester and turned in for an early night, knowing that the turmoil in his mind would deny him sleep for hours despite his tiredness.

***

The following day Frank clocked in for his shift at a machinery warehouse further north in Woodford after as much sleep as he anticipated. Two hours at most. The work was mind-numbingly dull but it paid a few bills. Frank stepped into a small, claustrophobic office where another man sat slumped in a chair, a bank of CCTV monitors in front of him and the room reeking of takeaways and human sweat.

"Morning, Toby. Jesus, it stinks in here," said Frank, covering his mouth and nose with a glance of his palm.

"A New Year present for you, Frank," said the younger man, grabbing his phone and wallet from a side table and standing up with a sudden eagerness to leave. "You're too kind," said Frank with undisguised sarcasm.

"Oh yeah, the boss man said he wants a word with you this morning. Guess he'll pop by?" Toby added with a half shrug.

"Oh right, thanks, Toby," Frank replied, curiosity mildly piqued.

The young man typed in a code to the console panel and left the security office with a slam of the door, leaving Frank alone to get on with his routine. Coffee first, then login to check the night's logs and take a first of several walkabouts to check the integrity of various exits and entrances inside and outside of the warehouse complex. Fifteen minutes later his employer, Mr Parkinson, walked in. He nodded to Frank.

"Morning, Frank. How's it going?"

"Not bad, thanks. Not bad. Toby mentioned you wanted to see me?"

Parkinson nodded, his face serious. "Yes, I'll not beat about the bush, then," he muttered, hesitating for a moment. "Your contract – the company are re-structuring a few things. The short of it is, I—"

Frank held up his hand, unable to listen to anymore. "My contract isn't being renewed?"

Parkinson sighed. "That's it. I'm sorry, Frank."

Frank shrugged. "It's the way it goes. Not ideal, but I'll find something else."

He had guessed it might be something like that with his contract renewal a few weeks away. There was no doubt it was a harsh blow to him and his plans to restore his relationship with his family, despite his outward show of nonchalance to Parkinson.

During his shift he had spoken to Maria but didn't mention the work situation. Time was needed to sort that out. Then he had checked in on the kids; Joe and Zak. Baby Zoe was barely a year old and gurgled in the background. He would have some time to spend with them at the weekend, he said, and genuinely looked forward to it. It was Thursday.

After the shift finished, Frank decided to stop in the pub on the way back home, the pull of downing a pint was just too hard to resist.

He left his car parked on the street and began the short stroll to the pub. In an old Vauxhall Astra opposite, Frank caught a brief glimpse of a semi-familiar face. Was that the guy that he'd seen opposite his flat? He was making a call inside the vehicle and it was difficult to get a clear view.

Same man? Frank sneaked another look as he continued on his way but couldn't be sure. What he did know was his senses were on full alert.

The pub was busy with the after-work crowd of punters desperate for some escapism at the bottom of a glass. A television relayed the news, the sound turned down while the closed captioning rolled over the bottom of the screen and a murmur of conversations, laughter and shouts filled the air. Frank was sitting away from the bar in a booth, the paper spread out in front of him, nursing a Guinness with a bourbon chaser on the side. He had positioned himself so that he had an eye on the door that he scanned every time it opened. Another familiar figure walked in and Frank instinctively lifted the newspaper higher to conceal himself.

"Hello, Frank."

He peeked from behind the paper to see a familiar Afro-Caribbean face. The long dark coat, open at the buttons revealing a crisp suit and tie underneath. The epitome of a smart, hard-working businessman – maybe a debonair playboy or an aspiring entrepreneur, born to hustle. Except the face looking at him was worn and tired-looking. A stark contrast to the well-turned-out attire.

"Marcus? I thought it was you. This is a coincidence," Frank said evenly, knowing it wasn't.

Marcus gestured to the seat opposite. "May I?"

Frank nodded and folded up his paper as Marcus eased into a chair. Frank noticed the man in the black leather jacket entering the pub door before moving to the bar.

"How have you been keeping?" Marcus asked, keeping the conversation light.

Frank looked at him for a moment, pausing, wondering what this was all about.

"Well, it's been better. How goes the world of *Liberatus News*?

"Good. Yes, good."

Frank jerked his head at the man at the bar. "Who's your friend?"

Marcus glanced over and then caught Frank's level stare, a moment of embarrassment flashed across his face as if caught out with a hand in the piggy bank.

"Ah, you noticed."

Frank waited, taking a sip of his pint, forcing the explanation.

"He's security. A private detective hired by me."

"To follow me? What's that all about?"

Marcus shook his head. "Don't take it personally. I needed to make sure of your routine. And check no one was shadowing you."

"There's been no-one except your friend. He's been shadowing me." Frank sighed, not sure of what to make of it. He cut to the chase, draining the bourbon. "What's going on, Marcus?" he asked, catching Marcus looking at the drink.

"Don't judge," Frank snapped, slamming the glass on the table.

Marcus shook his head and leaned forward, resting his elbows on the dark wood table.

"There's no judgment here. You want another one?" gesturing at Frank's glass.

Frank gave him a withering look that told Marcus where to go.

"Look, I have a message from John. All I can say is," Marcus glanced around the pub, "he wants to talk to you, urgently."

Frank let out a snort of derision. "I don't owe him or you anything," he snapped.

Marcus studied Frank's face. "Look, I know I fucked up when it came to Pandora Red but lessons have been learned. You're needed, and you'll be well paid. At least hear me out?"

Frank leaned back and sipped his pint. "Not interested," he snapped.

Marcus kept his face impassive but Frank could tell he was reeling inside. He surely couldn't have thought it would have been that easy. After all that happened? It would be hard for Frank ever to forget. When Maria and Joe had been held captive by the criminal Viktor Kozel under the orders of David Devlin, the MI6 head at the time, Marcus Brady had royally screwed up. Frank had told Marcus to hold back the information from publication for three days to give him enough time to track down Maria and Joe to save them from execution. Yet *Liberatus News* had published the revelations about Operation Oculus – a massive surveillance programme a whole day early.

A mistake that had very nearly cost his family their lives.

Marcus Brady's pathetic justifications had been that "the police had raided their offices", "the staff and journalists harassed" and "they had been followed by the authorities".

The PI had moved from the bar to sit a table close to the front window and stole the occasional stealthy glance towards them.

"You can tell your man his job is done. It's not happening, Marcus. I'm trying to restart my life, away from all that shit." It was true, partly. On the one hand he wanted to look out for his family and be there for them. A steady, safe job could win Maria back. Convince her that his old yet brief life with the Dark State was over. On the other hand, there was the numbing mindlessness of a "safe job" just like the one he'd lost. He felt the pull of excitement associated with the very same world he just disavowed bubbling just under the surface and tried to dismiss it as a risk not worth taking.

Marcus placed his hands, palms down, on the table and dropped his head. "Alright. Your decision." He rose to stand, then buttoned up his coat.

"There's a time factor involved in this one. So if you change your mind, make sure you do it by Sunday." There was now a more authoritative tone in his voice as if he was no longer bothered by what Frank decided. He tossed down a business card in front of Frank.

"Just in case you lost my number," he said.

Then Marcus was gone with the PI quickly following him out of the door.

Chapter 4

After leaving the pub Frank headed over to the family house in Islington and slipped through the front door, immediately hearing the excited patter of feet. Zak appeared, peeping around the kitchen door, and Frank crouched, giving him a broad smile. "Hey, little man."

Zak's face broke into a delighted grin and he ran to his father who scooped him up with his hands, holding him high over his head. Frank screwed up his face in a mock grimace that always delighted the boy.

"Back here!" It was Maria shouting from behind the door. Frank carried his second son through the corridor to the back of the house. There was a screech as Frank entered the kitchen and Maria was comforting baby Zoe who was not happy about something.

"Oh, that doesn't sound good."

She gave him a knowing smile as she patted the baby on the back, rocking her to and fro.

"Another sleepless night. She's teething, I think," replied Maria.

Frank put Zak down who immediately scurried across to his toys that were piled up in the dining area of the extended kitchen.

"Where's Joe?"

"Football."

"Oh, right," he muttered, not hiding his disappointment. Maria gestured with a jutting of her head to a letter on the table. "That came through."

Frank picked it up and opened it. As he read it, his expression turned to a frown as he saw red lettering embedded in the text.

"What's this?" he asked even as he read the words from the mortgage company.

"Repossession threats," said Maria, with a hint of anger in her voice. Little Zoe had calmed and gurgled as Maria placed her in a baby recliner.

"Dammit. Payment of £3500 due immediately?" He read the rest of the letter.

"Well, they say if the arrears are paid, they will not go ahead with the repossession," said Frank hopefully.

"Oh well, that's alright then," Maria muttered, sarcastically.

Frank sighed and put down the letter as Maria moved to the back of the kitchen to put on the kettle.

"Look, don't worry about this I'll find the money," he said, not entirely convinced. He had some cash put by, and his current employers still owed him a month's pay. But after that, he had no idea how to make ends meet. "Paying rent on my place doesn't help," he added, flatly.

"I know but I think this is for the best right now. I don't want to go over it all again."

She slumped down opposite Frank, her face strained by conflicting emotions.

"I'm not going over anything again. Just pointing out some practicalities," he muttered. "Look, we'll sort something out. Don't worry."

Just then Frank's mobile chirped in his pocket. He fished it out and looked at the caller ID. It was from Ireland.

"Mr Hales. This is O'Farrell from Unicorn Estate Agents."

"Ah yes. Hello." Frank stood up and walked back to the corridor away from the kitchen.

"I'll cut straight to the chase. I'm afraid the owner has rejected your offer but he indicated that if you could stretch to fifty, he would be happy to talk."

Frank felt his stomach turn and sighed.

"OK, thanks for letting me know. Like I said, that was my best offer. Leave it with me anyway but I think it'll be a struggle." It was true. He was stretching things to snapping point as it was. Perhaps this wasn't the best time to be attempting to buy property.

"Alright, so. I'm sorry 'bout that. They're digging their heels in on this one," O'Farrell muttered in a sympathetic tone.

"Keep me in the loop. Take care and thanks again for letting me know."

"Good luck, Mr Hales."

Frank cut the connection and swore aloud – his dream had evaporated with that one call. It seemed that all his plans would have to be put on hold.

***

Frank stared at Marcus Brady's card.

The man very nearly put his family in their graves with his mistake of publishing the Oculus revelations early.

It was a good reason not to trust anything he said in Frank's book. And yet over the past twelve months, Frank's anger had dissipated. He would never forgive him entirely, but Brady had apologised, more than once. It was just a mistake, a human error. It wasn't as if they had to be best mates. John Rhodes he could respect but Brady – not so much.

Thinking back to that time brought Frank's thoughts around to Carl Paterson. He had never quite forgiven Carl for the way things had turned out after Cuba. The former MI6 man, now heading up Ghost 13, had been "economical with the truth" when it came to "Whisper Hunt" and, to some degree, the kidnapping of Maria and their eldest, Joe.

Still, he had merely been playing his role. A job not envied by Frank in the slightest.

He glanced back toward the kitchen as Maria took some milk from the fridge and he saw her cast him a brief look. Unjudging and trusting.

There could be severe consequences if he made this decision.

It was a curious paradox. Would Maria hate him for going back into the world of shadows? It was likely.

Yet, if he did this. *If.*

Then there was a real possibility he could set them all up for life.

Make them safe.

And he kept wondering whether he was behaving recklessly. Was he unconsciously rolling the dice to get back at Maria?

Yes, he had children to think about, but she would take care of them, of that there was no doubt. He did not dare analyse or speculate what could happen. A million different possibilities lay ahead.

But one thing was certain – once again he would be a mere pawn to be manipulated by the serious players lording it from above; all with agendas in a world where deaths were just part of a numbers game. Influential figures in the shadows pulling strings from the comfort and safety of their old boys' club armchairs with the aroma of cognac and cigar smoke filling the air of their cloistered environment. With all that he faced he knew there was only one thing to do.

He walked into the front room, typing in Brady's number as he went and then closed the door behind him.

Chapter 5

Frank stepped inside the cafe that was tucked away alongside the train tracks running into Gare du Nord, the central Parisian railway station. It had been a quick journey from St Pancras, through the Channel Tunnel. Inside, the cafe had high ceilings with ornate fixings and a large tiled wall blocking the kitchen. The daily menu was scribbled incoherently on a blackboard and, behind the counter, the coffee machine hissed and gurgled.

A young woman standing behind the service counter gave him a warm smile and asked him what he wanted to eat.

Frank only ordered a black coffee before moving deeper into the cafe, with decorated walls of old black and white framed photographs depicting a bygone Paris. He scanned along the sofas and low seating placed along the walls, then recognised a tanned Rhodes with his white hair near the back in a circular booth.

It was quiet, and there was no-one within earshot.

Rhodes looked up and smiled at seeing him.

"Frank!"

"Good to see you, John."

They shook hands and Frank sat down.

"Bienvenue à Paris," Rhodes added in a mock French accent.

"You're based here now?" Frank asked.

Rhodes shook his head. "Good God, no. I move around a lot – you know that."

Frank nodded, getting just the vague answer he expected. He guessed after Rhodes became a target a year before, ending in a nasty car crash, that he'd keep the details light. The man had nearly died and had carefully kept a low profile since.

Yet judging by this request for Frank's services, Rhodes was far from being done with his passion; the fight for greater liberty against the rising global state.

"So, I'm glad to see you're looking well. Keeping busy?"

Rhodes smiled. "Always."

After a few minutes of small talk, Frank sipped on his coffee while Rhodes leaned forward, his face becoming serious.

"I'm sure Marcus didn't give you too much information but you have to understand this is a delicate one. The usual reasons for discretion apply, of course. You understand?"

Frank nodded.

"I'm building a network to work on behalf of the people, not the State," Rhodes continued, "Someone who has important information and contacts, wants closer ties, perhaps a deal. This asset, let's call him 'Nero', wants to bring in his 'take' personally using his own method. Having said that, he's already sent some compelling samples of his merchandise. It looks like he's got pure 'glitter'. And that would be a massive coup for us."

"Glitter?"

Rhodes smiled ruefully. "Ah, an old intelligence term: 'information not yet understood or acquired.'"

Frank nodded while draining his coffee. "So, he's got intel for a media story that you are going to release?" he asked.

Rhodes shook his head. "No. Too early and too sensitive for that," he leaned back. "What I need you to do is rendezvous with Nero in Europe

– he's currently somewhere outside the US sphere of influence – then escort him to another location, nearer my base of ops. I need him there, on my team." Anticipating Frank's response, he continued, "he could just fly over but we need to be careful. The authorities have increased the monitoring of all global transport manifests so, as a precaution, I need you to babysit him. It's imperative you get him over there safely."

Frank's face remained impassive but, inside, he had doubts.

"Can you tell me where?"

"Right now, no. But you'll get the destination soon enough. I would estimate it'll be around a month's mission time."

Rhodes took out a tablet from his bag and tapped on the screen, then handed it to Frank who looked down at a young man in his late twenties with dark hair, a trimmed beard and the pronounced cheekbones of Anglo-Asian descent.

"So accompany this guy somewhere, destination yet to be confirmed."

"Yep."

"Will there be other interested parties involved? I need to know this, John." He observed Rhodes as the old man shook his head.

"No, as long as we're careful. Just communicate the way I tell you, don't take any chances. I'll give you more details as soon as you're ready. You'll get a phone, a legend ID and cash. Nero will be travelling as Mark Simpson."

Frank nodded slowly, looking at the face again.

The money for the job would certainly help him get that farmhouse in Ireland, perhaps even get his family back together. But he sensed something was off. He had a lot of questions that needed answering.

Rhodes seemed to read his facial expression. "You'll get all the info you need soon. Just think of the money, Frank," Rhodes scribbled down a figure on a piece of paper, then slid it over to Frank, who glanced at it.

"It's pretty good 'Fuck you' money. You could do something good, maybe even buy property—"

Frank glanced at him sharply, wondering if he knew about Ireland. He didn't want anyone to know about that. Not just yet.

"Have you been in touch with Maria?"

Rhodes took the tablet back and tapped on the screen as he spoke. "Maria? No, I've had no contact with her at all. Why?"

Frank regarded him with interest. He seemed genuine enough.

"Just wondered. We've separated," Frank heard himself say. He wasn't sure why.

Rhode's face changed to concern and he looked at Frank with sympathetic eyes. "Oh God. I'm sorry, Frank. Really sorry. What—" he stopped himself and finished, "none of my damn business."

Frank waved a dismissive hand. "Not something I thought would happen either. But with this line of business—"

Rhodes held up his hand and nodded with understanding.

"I know, I know – I have a family too, as you know – it's difficult."

Frank glanced out towards the street and sighed. Deep down he had already made the decision and was now teetering on the edge of making the commitment.

So, let it begin.

Chapter 6

Carl Paterson had never felt so on edge. He downed a whiskey to calm his inner turmoil and leaned forward, feeling the amber liquid burn the back of his throat as he gestured to the flight attendant for another.

A new world order would see the end of intelligence institutions such as MI6, CIA and the rest, of that Carl had no doubt. It might take twenty years, maybe fifty? He simply didn't know. But his instinct was telling him it was coming and Carl wanted a legacy to reflect his true worth. It had been bloody hard work building up his enclave of power since being given the opportunity to head up the Ghost 13 estate. He had rapidly nurtured a small group of assets, scouts as he called them, and now he wanted to expand that as quickly as possible.

If there was any hint of truth in this rumour, all that he had built could be swept away in less than the blink of an eye. His network, his power, everything, which was why he was heading to the Buckley Air Force Base in Colorado to get clarification, under the guise of a fact-finding mission. G13COMM had already been set up in the US under Colonel Wexhall's command. The next item on the agenda was the take over of Carl's UK operation. What that might mean for Carl he had no idea.

Carl turned his gaze from the flood of endless cloud outside the aircraft to the dog-eared book laying on his fold-out table, the one he carried around in his briefcase along with his work files. It was a welcome distraction and he picked it up once again. It was an in-depth historical account that focused on the first secret agent network in England during the reign of Elizabeth I. In recent years he had turned to history as a conduit for knowledge.

History repeated itself, so the cliché said. But it was true.

The world of the Elizabethan court fascinated him and kept his mind occupied on those occasions when he needed to push his work worries out of his head.

He flipped open the book to his last read page.

Robert Cecil had inherited the spy network from his father, William Cecil, the man who had entrapped Elizabeth's sister, Mary Queen of Scots, and then ultimately condemned her to death for her plot to become Queen of England. Despite his intention to protect Elizabeth, it had got him banished from the court for his trouble. Robert, now first secretary to the queen, already having been brought up learning the spycraft and the extent of his father's extensive network, had spies everywhere. His rival for the queen's ear in the court, the Earl of Essex, was an athletic man with many victories in battle under his belt. This was a direct contrast to Robert, who was hunchbacked which gave him the demeanour of a crouched toad, and as such was nicknamed 'pigmy' by the queen.

One of Cecil's spies, Lopez, the queen's doctor, had been accused by Essex of plotting to poison the queen. Cecil had considered whether or not to stand up for one of his own but ultimately deemed it too dangerous to intervene on Lopez's behalf. Cecil's own future goal to become the ears and eyes for the queen was at stake, and so he did not stand in the way of the doctor's execution despite knowing he was innocent.

Carl took a pause, sipped his drink and looked back out at the flat blanket of cloud. The sun rays were lighting up the top of them.

He did what had to be done. To protect his network. Smart.

Carl continued reading.

As Elizabeth came to the end of her life, it was apparent that there was no natural successor, except the Protestant King James of Scotland (The son of Mary Queen of Scots). Fearing James would hold the death of his mother against him, who had been condemned by Robert's father, the private secretary knew he had to tread very carefully indeed.

When Essex, having fallen out with the queen, attempted a coup with 200 men (backed by King James), it was Cecil's spy network that ensured it was crushed. Essex was executed on the 25th of February 1601. On hearing that the coup had been unsuccessful, King James approached Cecil, sounding him out on whether Cecil would act as James' eyes and ears in the queen's court.

This could easily have been a set-up in this era of intrigues and treasonous plots. It was a dangerous time for Cecil, so he took extra precautions and waited before giving a response to the Scottish monarch. When he did eventually reply he did so through a coded proxy by diplomatic cover so his direct contact would not implicate him. He told James to wait it out.

When Queen Elizabeth passed away on 24th March 1603, Cecil oversaw the succession of King James to the throne, while retaining his own power base.

Carl put down the book and sipped his whisky. It was a compelling parallel. In some ways, he saw himself as Cecil. A man who needed to be smart to survive, and keep an eye on the board pieces at all times.

His thoughts returned to his own situation.

Stay calm, Carl. Let's see what the wind smells like in Colorado and hope it doesn't smell like shit.

***

After around thirty minutes of waiting, Carl tossed his plastic coffee cup into the nearby bin and slumped back into the plastic and chrome chair, absolutely seething. The intermediate US official had kept him waiting as if he were some lowly civil servant. He could do without this bureaucratic posturing, but there would be no complaining on his part. Subtle shifts were happening in the global intelligence community, and Carl needed to step carefully to make sure he was still standing after the flux.

A major appeared finally.

"Mr Paterson. The colonel will see you now."

Carl stepped inside a sparsely furnished office and saw Wexhall in military fatigues behind his desk talking into a phone. Wexhall acknowledged him with a nod and Carl waited for the call to end, shifting his weight from one foot to another. He focused on a world map behind the colonel, wondering where on the globe he intended to stretch his tentacles.

He slammed the phone down.

"Mr Paterson. Please sit down."

Pleasantries over in a flash, the colonel cut to the chase.

"Listen, Carl. We all heard about what happened to your boys over in Cuba, the leaks and red faces. The boys at the top of the tree getting caught with their paws in the cookie jar."

Carl remained impassive, barely holding down a boiling frustration. This meeting was going exactly as he thought it would.

"It was regrettable. Impossible to predict that our top line could be compromised. Lessons have been learned."

Wexhall placed his elbows on the table, leaning forward.

"The fact that the head of MI6 was running his own show, bringing in assets isn't what bothers me about this. What bothers me, is he got caught."

Carl could feel himself shrinking in his seat and barely hid a flash of contempt on his face.

"The Ghost 13 Command is expanding whether you like it or not. Military and intelligence wings sitting outside of the power of individual governments. A more global approach. That means your little set-up will soon be coming under our umbrella. We need to work together, Carl."

"I understand the nature of the restructuring. I've seen the brief," said Carl sternly.

"So, my big question is – do I *really* need you? Can your network deliver? Can *you* deliver? I'm not sure I've seen anything that convinces me that's at all possible," Wexhall growled in a tone that matched Carl's.

Carl drummed his fingers on the side of the chair.

"Well, that clarifies things, but I have to warn you that any shakeups right now are going to have a direct effect on current operations," Carl warned, "We have assets in the field and rocking the boat right now could put lives at risk. It would be a problem."

Wexhall seemed to be thinking as he swung round in his chair to face the window.

"Y'know what would be useful, Carl? Little eyes and ears inside a certain 'group of interest' based over on your side of the pond." Wexhall shot Carl a glance and swung back round to face him. "What have you got on Liberatus?" he added the question, heavy with hidden meaning.

"They've been on our radar for a long time. The news media side has been a pain in the authorities' backside for many years. The founding CEO, John Rhodes, worked for our side once, but now we believe he's building a rogue intelligence network, so definitely a person of, or should I say a group of interest—" Carl paused, assessing if the colonel had anything to add but Wexhall said nothing, so he continued. "His brother founded Goya Tech in Silicon Valley. They have some consumer tech products, they're behind some of the Internet's most progressive tools but have been putting out feelers regarding government contracts both here and in Europe."

Wexhall rested his head back on the chair rest, seemingly bored with the assessment. "So, Liberatus could be seen as a potential internal threat in your country," he said, sharply.

"We've crossed swords before now," replied Carl, his mind returning to the messy Operation Whisper Hunt, and the subsequent Liberatus exposure of the Oculus programme.

Wexhall straightened up. "So then, it might be seen as beneficial to both our interests to have an asset inside their organisation?"

"Right, I see where this is going."

"Then see it goes somewhere; deliver me something I can actually use, Paterson, otherwise you're out."

Chapter 7

Carl Paterson had to stay at the hotel near Denver airport for the flight back. He checked in and went to the restaurant, sitting alone in one of the corners, slowly destroying a rare filet mignon steak with methodical precision. A Cabernet Sauvignon complemented it perfectly. Foolish not to take advantage of a generous expense account. The perks associated with this job had been tremendous from the beginning. Even Percy Braithwaite, the man who had helped set up Ghost 13, had always made that clear: everything was off the record. No official salary, no pension. All that would be provided by means of employment by SIS (The Secret Intelligence Service) or MI6 as they were better known. If he wanted holidays, cars; it was all provided by the Service including access to the various plushly furnished apartments dotted around the country.

As he finished patting his mouth with an Irish linen napkin, he felt his phone vibrate in his pocket and decided to ignore it, nodding to the waiter to order the blueberry cheesecake and double cream instead. He would enjoy his meal first before fielding any calls. The meeting hadn't been a great experience. What was it Wexhall had said? "The Ghost 13 Command is happening whether you like it or not." That riled him but at least it confirmed where he stood. His place in the new order was threatened, absolutely no doubt about that.

Have to play it carefully, he thought. Make every move count. Think like Cecil.

After the coffee and cake been placed in front of him, Carl pulled out his phone and read an encrypted message with a wry smile. It was one of his operatives back in London with news of his old mate, Frank Bowen.

***

Frank buttoned up his jacket to keep out the biting harshness of the wind and jammed his hands back in his pockets as he hurried down the Edgware Road. Either side, the darkened buildings reminded him of cut-outs used in the backdrop of a theatre stage. Overhead, the sun struggled to break through a blanket of high cloud bleaching out the sky, completing the effect.

He had accepted the job with Rhodes and was about to step on stage. What new drama skulked behind the curtain exactly?

Gotta keep that shit out of your head. Focus on the job, Frank.

And he would have to sell it to Maria. Doing this kind of work was precisely why they had separated in the first place. Should he lie to her?

Frank crossed the street outside Paddington Green Police Station, weaving around the slow-moving traffic in the direction of the tube station. A siren faded against the background city hum.

Obviously he couldn't give her any details, or even say that it was working for Rhodes. She might even support that, having worked for him before. But he was still putting himself and his family on the line, no matter which way he could spin it.

No lying. Frank would be effectively lying to his kids in that sense too. Zoe and Zak were too young to be anything but accepting of what their dad told them. But Joe, he'd also ask questions.

Frank sensed rather than saw a black Chevrolet 4X4 pull onto the double yellow lines just a few yards ahead of him and focused on it. Then a familiar figure got out. Bald, squat with beady eyes that focused on Frank. The man was already moving towards him.

Carl Paterson's rottweiler.

Just then, strong hands grabbed his arms from both sides.

"Don't run anywhere, Frank." A gruff voice from his left.

He turned to see the culprit, long grey hair, unshaven with a smell of cigarettes and body odour. On his right, another big thug with close-cropped ginger hair wearing a grey bomber jacket.

"Hardly likely, is it?" he hissed.

They were pushing him towards the car while the bald one gestured to the open rear door of their 4x4.

"Carl just wants a friendly chat," he said, casually.

Right in front of the police station. Cheeky bastards!

***

Carl Paterson was waiting for Frank in Hyde Park. The place didn't evoke the rosiest of memories after their little dispute there but Frank guessed Carl was fond of it.

His rottweilers had searched him in the car and scanned for any concealed electrical devices before they drove up towards Marble Arch. At least he didn't have the phone that Rhodes had given him for their initial comms. He wondered if more thugs from the firm were breaking down his flat door at that very moment, slashing open his mattress and throwing his clothes onto the floor.

Bald thug and ginger lad walked with him across the park. The other man stayed in the vehicle.

Frank caught sight of Carl drinking out of a paper cup huddled against the outside bar of a permanent snack hut that had its back to Serpentine Lake. Cold blasts came in off the water that cut through to the bone as grey clouds drifted overhead.

Baldy nodded in the direction of Carl.

"Have your chat. Don't be a prick and try anything stupid," his accent gruff and Northern.

Frank's recent conversions with Rhodes echoed in his mind as he approached Carl. The gravity of this didn't need underlining. He took a deep breath and sidled up next to his one-time good friend. It was just the business. The way of things, now. The days of them sharing their private thoughts over a pint seemed a long time ago.

"Well, Carl, you goin' to get me one?"

Carl glanced up and offered a thin smile, his features hagged, chin, unshaven.

"Of course. You still drinking it straight and black?"

"Thanks."

Carl added to the order and they took their drinks.

"Let's get out of this bloody cold, huh?" muttered Carl. Hunched like an old woman he started to scurry to a wooded section that offered a bit more shelter. There was a line of tables with the hardcore smokers braving the elements. They placed their paper cups on a vacant table but didn't bother to sit down.

"Well, I wasn't expecting to see you again," Frank said.

Carl was staring across the lake beyond Frank's shoulder and his eyes turned to him.

"I know. Neither was I. But such is life..."

"Look, it's all water under the bridge. Right? We both had our reasons to be angry. I don't want to rake over old grass again."

Carl nodded in agreement. "So, any guesses why you're here?"

"—because your merry pack of lap dogs dragged me off the street? Dunno, mate."

Carl's eyes seemed to grow colder, more focused.

"I know you're working for Rhodes and his little band of fucking ingrates."

So, he knows. Or was it a trick?

"Rhodes? Why would I want to go near him – or any of that other again?"

"I don't know, Frank. You tell me. Why would you want to? Trust me, I know you've met up with him. I heard Paris is nicer in the spring. No idea why you'd want to go there this time of year."

Frank let out a long sigh. "You've been watching me?"

"Him. Naturally. "

Carl blew on the hot coffee and risked a sip, followed by a facial expression of regret.

"What do you want?"

Carl turned away from Frank and glanced over at his two men, who were now sitting on a bench a few metres away.

"I need eyes and ears, that's all. Just keep me in the loop. I don't know what he's asked you to do, but I can make life very difficult if you get my drift?" There was a subtle tone of threat, then became more upbeat. "But you'll be compensated. Something extra for the family."

Frank felt his temperature rise a fraction at the mention of Maria and the kids.

"What are you getting at?"

"Now, now don't be touchy. I'm doing you a favour. You remember the old place, huh? Come and see me. The sooner, the better."

He gave Frank a friendly slap on the bicep and moved off.

"You're just a ladder man, Carl," Frank said, flatly. It was a derogatory term for anyone in the intelligence community that climbed the career ladder with a cold indifference to their colleagues.

Carl gave a snort of derision. "Good to see you again, Frank," he added before moving off around the shack.

Chapter 8

G13COMM, Buckley Air Force Base, Colorado

Wexhall kneaded his football-shaped stress ball in a quick continuous rhythm as if he were replicating his own heartbeat. A light rain pattered against the office window behind the drawn blinds providing background noise to his thoughts on the Brit – Carl Paterson.

The whole agency was now up and running, albeit in skeleton form. The next stage would be to establish satellites in Europe and naturally its namesake in London would be an important hub. But as Wexhall had stated so plainly, whether Carl Paterson would be "head honcho" over in Britain was very much in the balance.

Wexhall placed the stress ball aside and sipped his coffee. Perhaps it would be interesting to see how Carl operated, whether he would step up and be useful. After all, the man's position was in Wexhall's hands, and he knew it. Wexhall and his associates had worked damned hard to bring this about – there could be no weaknesses tolerated in the machine.

An incoming message on his console brought him back to the present. Wexhall stared at the notification as he ran the decryption and waited for the message to appear. It was from his CIA insider at Langley.

Possible Darkwood compromise. Recommended you check for leaks, no other info known.

Wexhall grimaced. This would put everything he had worked for in jeopardy. It was frustratingly brief but told him enough. He closed the window, stood up and left his office, heading down the long corridor inside the temporary unit. Inside another adjacent space a skeleton staff were sitting in front of a bank of screens. The blond-haired sergeant major came to the door of an internal private office and saluted him.

Wexhall went inside and closed the door.

"Sergeant Major Stark. Pull up everything on Operation Darkwood. I need an overview right now."

Stark returned to his sunken chair and began typing on his keyboard. The colonel pulled up a chair and sat down next to him.

The screen revealed the Ghost 13 emblem for a moment before it evaporated as he logged into a secure interface.

The sergeant major turned to face Wexhall. "What do you need, sir?"

Wexhall gestured to a file symbol at the top right of the panel.

"I want a list of everyone involved in 'Darkwood' or have ever seen eyes on any aspect of the plan above security clearance level two. Give me a print-out."

"That will be in the hundreds, sir."

"I know, just do it."

A series of page icons flashed on the screen as the section of that document was sent to print, and the process began with a quiet rapid humming from the printer. The colonel grabbed the sheets one by one as they spat out onto the metal tray. After he was satisfied he had them all, he turned to leave.

"Alright, sergeant major, shut it down. Thank you."

He returned to his own office and laid out the sheets of paper across his desk. Then he poured himself a coffee and stared down at the faces. These were all people involved in the setting up of infrastructure for the new covert agency. Any one of them could be the source. He would need to roll up his sleeves and carry out a thorough investigation.

***

Tech analysis had isolated a timeframe and location of the data breach. It whittled the list down considerably. A large amount of data had been transferred inside K-section on the date in question, and that had given Wexhall a red flag list of five names. These were trusted employees, carefully sourced to help implement the backbone of the G13COMM set-up. It was hard to believe anyone inside would compromise them, let alone the people on this list. Precautions had been taken backed up by high salaries, and of course harsh consequences for any disloyalty.

He picked up the phone, spoke for a few moments then left for the interrogation rooms.

***

Wexhall watched the woman's eyes dart over in his direction through the dark glass two-way mirror in the wall. She looked scared.

Rightly so.

She was hooked up to a lie detection machine and had been asked a seemingly endless list of questions. The young blonde interrogator glanced up from his file, his emotionless voice tinny through the sound system inside the observation box.

"Ms Gilmore, thank you for your time," he said. Wexhall smiled at that. As if she had any choice.

"You understand that in cases of security breach situations we need to make thorough investigations," Stark continued. "You may return to your post."

The woman smiled, relief evident on her face and she stood up, brushed her hands down the front of her skirt and left the claustro-phobic, windowless room.

Wexhall depressed a button on the small panel next to the mirror.

"Thank you, sergeant major. We'll take a short break, then get the last name in." Stark acknowledged him with a nod and stood up, stretching his back.

The colonel remained in the small observation room alone, watching through the fishbowl mirror as Stark left to get a coffee. He took a seat at a small table, clutching the list in his bear-like hands and ran a pen through Ms Gilmore's name. The lie detector was the most accurate gauge of the truth available to them. The alternative method would have been of a more persuasive nature. But that method, Wexhall knew full well, would be extremely difficult to carry out on American citizens on home soil even if they were working inside military intelligence. The fact that it even crossed his mind crystallised to the colonel how desperate he was to plug this hole.

He would have to tread carefully and avoid stepping on any shards.

After a few minutes, Stark returned with a mug of coffee and glanced in Wexhall's direction, as if waiting for the order. He was the only one Wexhall could trust it seemed. A loyal, dependable and faithful soldier.

Wexhall leaned forward and depressed the microphone control. "Sergeant Major Stark. Let's get this-—" Wexhall glanced down at the last name on the list, "Bradley Meers in and see what he has to say."

Stark picked up the phone, spoke for a few moments and then left the room. He returned with a short, thin man in his forties with a balding pate and unsure demeanour, apparently surprised and afraid of what might be coming. Wexhall recognised him as a member of the signals unit, those responsible for the integration of all the G13COMM systems at Buckley Air Force Base, Colorado. According to the file before him, Meers had worked for the NSA before being approached by one of Wexhall's staff to work on Operation Darkwood around six months ago. His login keycard had been recorded online at the exact time that the sensitive data had been copied to a remote device.

Wexhall leaned back, bristling with anticipation as he watched Stark hook up Meers to the lie detector and proceed with the questioning. He had left the best one to last in part to savour the moment; as if saving a cookie until after lunch.

Stark ran through a list of basic questions establishing his identity, age and address and other criteria, a monotonous routine he could blitz through in his sleep before getting to the matter in hand.

"You were here, working as normal on the third of January. Is that correct?" Stark asked evenly.

"Er, the third?" Meers wiped the back of his neck, glancing at the mirror like they all had, wondering what their fates might be. "Yeah, I was in, sure. I've never been off since I started, except weekends and the Christmas holiday of course."

"Between 12–14.30 on that date we have your login ID as online at the same time that there was a data breach. This corresponds with your access level – a grave offence, Mr Meers."

Meers clasped his fingers together on the table, fidgeting, eyes wide as he took in the accusatory tone of the questioning.

"No, that's absolutely not true. I have never breached any rules or done anything I wasn't supposed to be doing."

"Do you feel loyalty to your previous agency, the NSA, Mr Meers?"

"Well – I – they were my employer, just doing my job there, enjoyed it but no I don't consider—"

"So what we have here," Stark cut in, "is that you were logged onto the Ghost network, level five at the same time as this breach. How do you explain that?"

"As I said, I didn't do anything wrong – I can't explain," he trailed off, the anxious expression turning to a frown as he struggled to remember. "Wait. Let me think, that date is familiar actually. It was the first Monday after the holidays, right?"

Stark didn't even need to blink. "Correct."

Meers looked more confident as the memory returned. "Yeah, Monday, right. I remember because it was Susan Gilmore's birthday, from our team. You can check that. Someone had arranged a quick and dirty birthday cake with the kitchen staff. We arranged to meet in the canteen, but one of the other guys popped his head around the door and asked me to come with him. I was a bit rushed and I'm afraid to admit I may have left my key card on my desk. Stupid, I know." He looked at Stark, resigned.

In the observation room Wexhall crossed his arms as he watched, slowly shaking his head.

"That should have been reported, Mr Meers. You left the keycard for how long?"

"Ah, an hour I guess. At least an hour – yeah – maybe more."

"Was there anyone else around in K Section that you noticed when you left?"

Meers brushed his hand over the bald dome, screwing his face up for a moment. "I know Clara was at her desk, over by the windows. Then that Asian guy, didn't know him too well – Tom Lee – I think?"

"He was where when you left?" Stark asked in a monotone voice.

"Just milling around, at his desk by the windows where he usually works."

Stark nodded and glanced towards the mirror at Wexhall for a moment, then continued the questioning. The colonel could see the detection graph was steady. It was highly unlikely this idiot was lying.

Meers wouldn't see out the rest of his contract – Wexhall would make sure of that. He'd be lucky not to get buried in the desert.

But now they had a name.

The Clara woman had already been cleared, and that left the last suspect – Tom Lee.

Time to get to work.

Chapter 9

Studio 31, Limehouse Cut

Frank parked up near the old grain warehouse, situated on the Limehouse Cut Basin, and the sight brought back mixed memories from only a year before. He buzzed the intercom access explaining his appointment. After walking up the circular metal steps, his footfall echoing up through the shaft-like space beneath him, Frank was met by a man he didn't know who offered coffee. Then he was ushered into a side room, sparsely furnished with a desk and a few chairs. An unused whiteboard was on the wall and a blind covered an internal window overlooking where Frank remembered the open-plan ops section was situated.

After a few minutes, Carl joined him, keeping it light with a handshake and a few words of small talk before easing himself behind the desk.

"Any old faces still here?" Frank asked, gesturing towards the window behind the blind.

"Ah, well. Keller's gone, replaced by my new superior. Griff and Harry are still holding on by their fingernails."

Frank nodded, wondering if Carl's thoughts had drifted back to the Pandora operation and regretted asking.

"Coffee good?" Carl asked, flipping open a folder in front of him.

Frank took a sip and smacked his lips. "Hmm, actually not bad."

"One of my numerous shake-ups to this operation."

"Our enemies must be quaking in their boots," Frank quipped. Carl's smile weakened.

"I'll put you on the payroll, give you the protocols, codes, identity, all that jazz. You need to keep me informed with regular updates. Any further word from Rhodes?"

Frank shook his head. "No, should be any day now."

Carl glanced at him and shut the folder.

"Alright, Harry will take you through the protocols. A few of them have changed since you were with us before. Then that's it."

Frank drained his coffee and made his way to the door.

"And, Frank—" Frank turned back as Carl stood up. "Do some press-ups or something for Christ's sake – you look terribly out of shape for a field op."

***

The hazy mists that had clung to the hills and small ridges of the Mendip Hills in the West Country had receded as Frank and Sam trooped up the path.

It'll clear in an hour Sam had said, and he was right.

It was a few hours drive from London, but as Sam was based in Cheddar, a small town bordered with hills, Frank decided it was worth the trip. The area was rich with wild plateaus, gorges, and calming stretches of water scattered around its hills, interspersed with peaks and thick woods.

"We'll take a run, sweat out those toxins. Just follow my lead," Sam said before breaking into a leisurely unforced sprint.

Frank followed, his large backpack clunking with the rocks inside and basic supplies. Both men had their ankles wrapped up tight with bandages to keep the risks of any sprains or breakages to a minimum.

Frank focused on the ground, his heartbeat setting a regular rhythm. In his mind he pictured himself as a machine – his legs were pistons that propelled him across the ground. He smiled, remembering a comic from when he was a kid – the numbskulls: about a group of miniature characters inside someone's head, directing their actions from their pilot cockpit.

Stupid, but a classic.

After a few miles, Frank felt his lungs burning – the recent lapse into booze and the occasional smoke all coming back to haunt him. The backpack seemed to weigh more than ever, and he wanted nothing more than to stop and lie down on the soft, inviting grass.

"Keep going!" Sam shouted as if reading his mind from afar. "Just pain – push through it," he added, almost certainly with a smirk.

"Fuck," Frank winced and gritted his teeth, "you."

The crest of the hill with a clump of rocks beckoned nearer – their rest point.

When they arrived, Frank threw the backpack onto the ground with a clunk and joined it there, gasping and spitting, sucking down air in greedy gulps.

He looked up at Sam, who remained on his feet with a slowly shaking head, tutting.

"There's work to be done, I see. Huh, Frank?"

He was right. Lots of work to be done and this was just the beginning – just the bare bones.

***

Frank stretched his calves under the table. The gruelling week of training with Sam had put him in much better shape, physically and mentally. He wanted to savour the remaining time with Maria before he dropped the bombshell.

Rhodes had sent word – he was to leave in two days.

The added element of Carl crashing the party was a real pain, but Frank cast it out of mind, for now. Time to think wasn't a luxury he had right now.

Maria finished a phone call, grabbed a carton of juice from the fridge and held it up at Frank.

"No, I'm alright."

She sat down and rested her elbows on the table top, fixing green eyes on him that silently questioned him. Joe was at school, Zak was in afternoon nursery and the baby was asleep in the kitchen cot.

"I'm gonna be away for a while."

"Where are you going?"

Frank glanced out through the old sash window that looked out against a red brick neighbouring wall. A ginger cat casually strolled along the top before jumping down on the far side.

"I can't say—"

Maria stood up.

"Oh for fuck's sake!" she blurted out.

"It's a case of being able to help you and the kids out. You want to stay here, don't you?"

Maria had her hands on hips and looked away from him as if he had insulted her.

"You're putting yourself in danger again, aren't you?"

When he didn't answer, she stared back at him, shaking her head.

"Why would you want to do that? What about the children? You want them to be fatherless or something?"

"It's not like that at all. I wish I could say, I really do, and give you more details, but—"

"Is it for Carl?"

Frank focused on the juice carton, the logo depicting a very happy orange cartoon as if it had won the lottery. He wanted to close his eyes when saying it.

Lies, bloody lies.

"No, the other team and that's all I can say. No more," Frank rubbed his eyes, "I'll be back in a month." he added.

She held her head down as if battered down by a cloak of disappointment, but the anger was gone as quick as it had manifested.

"The other team," she repeated slowly and began busying herself, picking up a stray bib that had fallen from the washing basket before clearing away dirty plates.

"What about Joe? You going to tell him you're off to Disneyland without him?"

Frank groaned out loud at the jibe. "It's work. He'll understand."

"And he'll be scared. It hasn't even been a year since he saw you deal with that Russian guy and take him out—"

"He didn't see me take him out."

"He heard it and saw the body under the towels. Look, he locks it up inside himself, won't talk about it, but all that must be affecting him."

Frank knew it was. How could it not be?

He stood up to leave.

"I never wanted any of that to happen—"

"And you saved us, of course. So we will always be in your debt, won't we?"

"You don't owe me anything." He stepped to the kitchen doorway.

"Frank—" she reached out her hand and held his arm. "Please don't go. I know we've had our shit to deal with and it's been difficult, but your children need a father."

He took her in his arms and they hugged.

"I know, I know," he whispered as he held Maria tight, nuzzling his face in her hair.

Chapter 10

Wexhall's office, just beyond the high fences that cordoned off the G13COMM area in the Colorado air base, overlooked a small road and the seemingly endless rows of barracks. The colonel adjusted the blinds and stared out for a few moments before taking a seat in his leather chair to go through the file on Lee.

His backlist included Blackwater, the private security company, specialising in corporate intelligence. No parents or family were known, but he had come highly recommended to G13COMM from every one of his employers.

They must have missed something. *Too clean.*

He picked up the phone and summoned Sergeant Major Stark.

Minutes later, Stark knocked and entered.

"Sergeant Major, change into civvies, take a specialist tactical team and go to Lee's house." Wexhall showed him the address on his screen which Stark memorised quickly. "See what you can find," the colonel continued, "in the unlikely event he stuck around, try to keep him alive."

"Sir!" Stark responded, snapping off a crisp salute before turning on his heels to leave.

Wexhall submitted Lee's details to various border agencies just in case he popped up on their radar. Then he launched the recently installed facial recognition software Face Glass with a few clicks.

He had managed to get early access to it from the military tech corporation, Cryostone. The biometric tool wouldn't roll out to the central intelligence and police agencies for years. Glitchy, for sure. Like a beta version of software thrown to the masses with a reluctant promise to fix the bugs later. Wexhall didn't care – he was determined to have fun with his new toy.

A photo of Tom Lee was loaded up, and Wexhall let it run – launching a fast-moving twin box next to the mugshot that flashed other faces with lightning speed.

He thought about Carl Paterson in London. Wexhall wondered whether to call on his services to help him out with all this? Carl's little operation was based nearer Europe – he had ears to the ground over there after all. Then Wexhall decided against it. Things might need to get nasty. It was his problem and his alone. Best keep it in the family and nip it in the bud.

***

Two teams.

Alpha one, a six-man unit, waited in the vehicle at the front of the single-storey condo in the leafy suburb of Thornton – their M-16's at the ready while the point man and breacher crouched by the rear doors. Stark waited with them, along for the ride. He was an efficient operator, and although fully trained in most military manoeuvres he would enter only once the house was deemed secure.

Around the corner, at a safe distance, were two more vans. The first held Alpha two, tasked with gaining access and securing the location with a waiting forensics team. The second held another crew, team Delta, acting as a comms centre.

"Alpha One Go! Alpha Two Go!" the crackle came across the comms from the command vehicle further down the street.

Simultaneously, a stream of heavily armed men clad in black fatigues and Kevlar helmets descended on the house in a snake – a single file to narrow the chances of being targeted. The teams moved on their objective with smooth efficiency, one moving to the rear of the building while the other took the front. There was a massive crunch as the first two men took care of the door breach with ruthless efficiency.

The point man went in first, stepping through the doorway into the hallway, a small kitchen visible at the end of the house. He stepped against the wall just outside the first left door to the living room that was shut firm. Another of the unit slowly opened it from the side. The point man, his M-9 sighted into the revealing space, quickly sliced the pie to the apex of the room to check for threats then moved to the left wall. He was followed by the other who covered the right with his M-16. To their right, an alcove connected to the dining room at the back.

Another two unit members peeled off to the right-hand side bedroom, mirroring the procedure.

"Front left, clear, Alpha Red proceeding to front back," came a voice through the comms.

A moment later. "Alpha Blue, front right, clear."

Another two men moved straight up the hallway to the kitchen in a crouch, weapons high, finding another empty space.

Moments later. "Alpha Green. Rear kitchen and bathroom clear."

A voice came through his earpiece, "House secure. No Tangos home. Over."

Stark holstered the sidearm he'd been holding while the tactical unit cleared the house, and picked up a small hard case box.

"Lionheart coming in. Forensics, meet me there," he replied and stepped out of the van into the cool breeze. Stark walked up the pathway and began to check each room carefully as the tactical unit prepared to leave. The team leader nodded to him as he entered the house.

"Are we done here?" he asked Stark.

"I'll take it from here, thanks, officer."

He walked through the rooms doing an initial scan, then placed the box down in the kitchen and called Wexhall on the mobile.

"Target has long gone, sir. I'll call in help from Forensics and see if we can find anything."

"Do that. Keep me posted."

Stark took out a pair of forensic gloves from the box and returned to the front living room. The house was sparsely furnished and devoid of any personal belongings, pictures or anything that gave a clue to Lee's character or lifestyle. He pulled on the gloves, stepped over to the sofa and crouched down beside it, running his steely gaze over the dark brown leather.

He spotted a small ripped section of plastic stuck out from one of the seams. It had probably been covered with a shrink-wrapped plastic sheet the whole time Lee had allegedly lived here to keep down on DNA leaks. He moved to a side cabinet and opened the drawers. Both empty.

Moving through the archway to the dining area, Stark saw a round glass table, with four chairs, neatly aligned as if they were in a showroom. Against the wall, a pine wood side cabinet contained just a stack of three plates. After making his way more thoroughly around the house, Stark had found nothing to take back to Wexhall.

"Sir?"

Stark turned to see two forensic investigators coming down the hallway.

"Give the whole place a good clean sweep and be quick about it."

The team set to work, unpacking their gear, while Stark went to check the outside perimeter.

***

From his peripheral vision Wexhall saw that the rapid movement on the screen had paused. He slid his chair closer.

"Sonofabitch," he muttered.

It was a match from security in Vienna airport. Wexhall scrolled through the details. Travelling under the name of Mark Simpson – the manifest had him on a flight to Las Palmas in the Canary Islands.

"Looking for a bit of sunshine are you, boy? What in the hell are you doing over there?" he said out loud.

Wexhall breathed out in satisfaction. They had a lead, at least.

Just then his phone buzzed. It was Stark.

"Tango left the building and he cleaned up well, but we found a print."

The fact that he had disappeared came as absolutely no surprise to Wexhall, but finding a single fingerprint might give them something. Was it fake? They had his biometric data on file including prints, taken during recruitment, so they'd soon find out.

"Alright. Bring it in and wrap it up."

Wexhall cut the call and stood up, pacing his office. It helped him think. He needed to check his assets in the field. He went to the wall safe, opened it up, retrieved a coded list and held it up to the light. The encrypted numbers, letters and symbols in columns indicated the different types of assets, their specialist skills, current locations and codenames. The colonel returned to his desk, typed into the decryption tool for a few minutes, then stared at the result. He had very few assets in the field. G13COMM were still in the process of putting together the infrastructure of the agency. His eyes settled on one –Elvira, currently based in East Europe, who could get there inside a day with any luck.

He checked some other options and decided on his original choice. He calmly activated the Ghost Order that would relay a coded message via phone.

Wexhall felt a glimmer of satisfaction. At least now one highly trained asset would soon be closing in to plug the leak permanently.

Chapter 11

Bratislava

Iskra Polyak codenamed 'Elvira', watched the snowflakes drift down from a bleak, dark sky to settle on the ledge of her sparse apartment window as she drained her espresso. Like a background ambience, the gentle hum of the fifty-year-old heating system had just kicked in. It was still dark outside, the yellow street lights revealing nothing more than the relentless snowfall. She was glad to be back in the warmth after her early run. Every spare moment she had outside of her work hours was used to hone her skills, keep herself in shape.

While she waited.

The small lean woman took a shower, then padded over to the kitchen alcove wrapped in a dressing gown and refilled her cup with more coffee. She found some eggs and began to whisk them up in a bowl. Methodically she chopped up some chorizo and onion, before adding a dash of spices, mixing them and pouring the yellow mixture into a butter heated pan.

As she began to eat the omelette she'd just made, her mobile phone started to vibrate on the worktop. Elvira picked it up and answered, listening to the short message, then ended the call.

Her wait was finally over.

It was a *Ghost Order*.

Elvira glanced at the clock: 3:48 AM.

She finished her food, washed up, dressed and began to go through the apartment, filling up a bin liner with anything she thought might compromise her identity or leave clues that might lead others to trail her – the bedsheets, items in the bathroom and cupboards. It didn't take long. Her wardrobe and clothes were kept to a minimum. Anything else in the apartment had come with the rental.

Her identity documents for her cover legend, Danika Klimer, had been kept in a waterproof bag and would now need to be ditched. It was just a case of wiping down any objects she touched often.

Less than an hour later she had dumped two bags in the bins in a quiet alley some way from her apartment, generously doused them in gasoline and left the burning trash behind her, smoke rising between the two buildings. She moved through the snow-caked streets, her fur-lined leather coat buttoned up tight, a white wool skull cap covering her dark hair and stepped onto a passing tram. She then watched the sparse streets rush by, figures in furry hats and heavy coats, heads bent down against the wind while making their way through the icy streets.

Her job, the bare old apartment, her identity – all fake – all make-believe. Would she miss Danika Klimer? She allowed herself a rare smile. How dull to have to clock into a deadly boring routine every day just for the privilege of paying a mountain of bills. No, she would not miss Danika or her job at the travel agency or the Slovakian capital that had been her sleeper station for almost a year now.

She exited the tram and headed toward the Nové Mesto district, turning off into a narrow road where grey housing blocks stood on either side. Apart from a dark figure crossing the deserted street, the neighbourhood had not woken up yet. That was good. Up ahead, she saw the trees from a little park, in the centre of the small housing estate, and turned in alongside, walking around its edge. She glanced back at her previous route, then into the empty park and slipped through a gate in the metal railings. Crunching through the fresh snow, Elvira reached a clump of trees that sprawled across the middle of the location. She glanced at her watch. The drop should have been made thirty minutes ago. Elvira moved to the children's play area at the rear of the park, behind a concrete public toilet, her eyes alert for any danger, then she spotted the mark – a symbol sprayed onto the side of the toilet block.

Confirmation.

Entering the play area, she slipped into a gap behind the toilet block and a fence then crouched down behind a large wheelie bin at the far end and pulled out a small backpack that had been stuffed underneath. She moved off quickly, throwing the pack over her shoulder as she headed towards the train station.

Chapter 12

Las Palmas, Canary Islands

Frank strolled along the promenade on the Playa De Las Canteras in Las Palmas, Gran Canaria. It was a warm evening, with just the right amount of breeze from the Canarias sea to feel warm and balmy. A handful of tourists and locals alike took in the evening air. A group of joggers padded by while out on the beach a middle-aged couple waded hand in hand out into the sea where fishing boats bobbed around like corks in the distance.

He had flown into Las Palmas the previous day, checked into a small apartment that Rhodes had provided and then met up with him in a park where the older man gave him his legend identity and other details.

Rhodes had delivered everything as promised and now Frank would be travelling as Frank Milligan, just another lone traveller making his way around the globe. Rhodes had even given him a large backpack to complete the illusion and established the final destination – Colombia. Mr Milligan was a researcher for the British Environmental Agency taking a sabbatical year, following his dream to travel to South America. The legend package Rhodes had given him included a passport for Milligan along with a driving licence as well as covert communication instructions and codes.

Colombia. All Frank knew about the country was it had been a narco drugs hell in the 80s but was supposedly a lot "safer now". That morning he had read through a background brief on the situation there. The drug cartels had wielded great power across the country, their tentacles of influence reaching the highest levels of government and police. It was apparent corruption would still be rife. Paramilitaries, both left and right wing, had caused a civil conflict that had lasted decades. FARC, the *Revolutionary Armed Forces of Colombia*, were a communist group operating a war against the Government since 1964 that used a kidnap for ransom policy as one of their tactics. They were also knee deep in the drug trade.

Then there was the National Liberation Army (ELN), regarded as being more politically motivated than the FARC. It had been responsible for hundreds of kidnappings and destroying infrastructure such as oil pipelines.

Another growing force was the United Self-Defence Forces of Colombia (AUC) – a right-wing umbrella group formed by drug-traffickers and landowners to combat left-wing rebel kidnappings and extortion.

The AUC, its roots in the paramilitary armies built up by drug lords in the 1980s, found influence from the military and some political circles. However, critics had denounced it as little more than a drugs cartel. Mix in numerous criminal gangs or *Bacrims* as the government and Colombia called them, and it still made for a perilous place to be in. Frank consoled himself that they would not be going to any of those dubious regions with Medellín being the end destination.

Frank turned off the promenade into one of the side streets, thronging with crowds all dressed up for the carnival. A continuous cacophony completed the backdrop: whistles, drumming and brass music drifted up from the streets that spiked inland.

He knew the hotel name where Nero was staying under the name of Mark Simpson – Hotel Canteras – given to him by Rhodes and decided to take a discreet look; check out his new friend from a distance.

It would be easy to have a few beers, check out a club; he was essentially single again, after all. But no time for that. Frank shook away the thought before it took hold. He needed to check out this guy as a priority, make sure there were no nasty surprises to be found or anything that might jump out of the shadows and bite him on the arse. Information is power and the more he knew about Nero, the better.

Frank arrived at the hotel, set on a corner of a busy road that housed bars and restaurants where the customers were already filling up the outside tables. He found a seat with a view of the hotel entrance and the street he had just walked down. He carefully watched the crowd of pedestrians walk across his field of vision as they headed for the seafront promenade. Just taking it all in while keeping his eyes open for anything that registered on his radar.

A waiter appeared, and Frank ordered a beer. For a moment he wished he had a cigarette. His gaze drifted to the hotel entrance where a few guests came and went. After twenty minutes of nursing his beer, satisfied no one was following him, Frank strolled over to the Hotel Canteras and into the busy lobby. It was an old building that hinted at the grandesque with fine-looking chaise longues and stylish furniture placed in the common bar area. A crowd of guests pushed past him, laughing and joking in Spanish. Frank glanced around, then took a seat on a couch in the bar area that faced the reception desk and surveyed the scene while ostensibly flicking through the menu. It was just due diligence; see what he could see for his own piece of mind if nothing else. After ten minutes the reception area became busy again, and Frank made his way to the elevators for the rooftop bar.

No one gave him a second glance.

The rooftop bar was crowded with festival goers warming up for the night's festivities ahead. Plush booths with low tables lined the edges. A bar was set in the middle, stationed by a smartly attired steward who was rushed off his feet with the relentless demand for wine and cocktails. At one end steel steps led to an outdoor Jacuzzi that appeared to be closed for the night and a balcony overlooking the lights of Las Palmas. Frank moved slowly around the rooftop, peering across at the city lights while discreetly checking faces among the party-goers. He casually circled the entire terrace, occasionally stopping while looking into the hidden nooks.

No sign of Nero.

It was as likely he would just have stayed in his room or gone out somewhere else. Frank leaned over the circular metal railings, watching the moon's reflection across the bay. In the distance, high spindly cranes were dark silhouettes, barely visible against a darkening sky.

What the hell was he doing here? The question came to mind out of nowhere. There was a moment of regret before he remembered his goals and reasons.

His family.

It's always for the family.

Even if Maria disapproved, which she did, but he couldn't blame her for that.

Frank glanced around again and recognised the figure coming down the steps from an upper balcony.

It was Nero, dressed in a blue short-sleeved shirt, jeans and holding a beer from which he took an occasional sip.

Frank waited for a moment, turning back to the view, then casually moved to the bar as Nero headed to the double glass doors back into the building, toward the elevators. Frank shifted away from the bar and followed Nero through the doors.

Frank checked his watch as he stepped back onto the busy street, back into the carnival. Just past eight. He followed Nero, wading through the crowds. Distant batucada drums drifted in and out from up ahead, while revellers with painted faces, masks and an assortment of wigs moved by in a blur. Up ahead, Frank could see the carnival floats, the bare flesh of dancers in tropical bird costumes gyrating to the drums.

Nero stopped at a makeshift stall and bought another beer, so Frank hung back on the opposite side, glancing around at the crowds while keeping an eye on Rhodes' new golden boy. Frank decided he would give it another twenty minutes, let Nero get on with his night then maybe even treat himself to a few hours to enjoy the carnival himself.

You're not on bloody holiday, Frank reminded himself, his professional training reprimanding him for entertaining such thinking.

A group of young women with feathered headpieces, linking arms, came down the street, singing loudly. A woman with blonde hair tied back in a ponytail, wearing a black T-shirt and backpack moved to the side of the road to let them pass. It was a young crowd, warming up for a long night of partying. The woman paused at a storefront and casually glanced over at Nero.

Frank's casual surveillance of his target seemed to have revealed a potential problem.

Nero moved off sipping his beer and nodding his head in time to the continuous drums, and the woman continued to shadow him, confirming Frank's suspicions.

Nero continued towards the *Parque de Santa Catalina*, all the roads leading to it seemed to create a bottleneck, where the crowds thickened considerably. The blonde followed. In the square, a giant Chinese dragon appeared, towering over the crowd, while a bleat of trumpets, drums and whistles punctured the atmosphere. Nero spoke to a few revellers outside one of the packed bars, accepting a few swigs of what looked like rum from the bottle. He seemed to be having a great time. Frank took a position by some benches, next to a group of party goers who were talking and laughing. He used them as cover to keep a subtle eye on both Nero and his new stalker.

Have to be careful here, Frank thought to himself. Be so easy to lose either one of them in this mayhem.

After ten minutes of socialising, Nero was on the move again, slowly making his way along the east side of the square before doubling back via a different street in the direction of the promenade. The blonde wasn't far behind, and Frank tried to keep them both in his sights at all times, but it was messy. There were too many people, and he found himself having to push through the bodies of tightly packed revellers to catch up.

It soon became clear Nero was returning to his hotel. Had enough partying perhaps? Through the packed crowd Frank saw that the woman had caught up and was speaking to him now, flicking her head back as she laughed at something.

Perhaps it was just his lucky night?

But something told Frank otherwise. She had tailed him for a fair distance, never letting him out of sight and had displayed all the signs of professional tradecraft.

What was he supposed to do? Call it in with Rhodes: 'Your man has a beautiful woman with him, and it looks like they are heading for his hotel room?'

Frank watched Nero and the blonde disappear through the doors of the hotel. As Frank walked in, he came up against a wall of carnival goers spilling out into the lobby from the packed bar. He spotted Nero at the reception desk waiting to talk to the desk clerk who was on the phone. His new friend loitered by the stairwell, seemingly keeping her face out of sight. Frank moved through the crowd, near enough to hear Nero order a bottle of bubbly to be delivered to his room, number 207, immediately. He then went to join the woman, and they disappeared up the stairwell, arm in arm.

What was her agenda, exactly?

There were two possibilities. Either it was just Nero's lucky night in which case what the hell was he doing here? The more likely one that Frank was increasingly convinced of was that this woman was a 'swallow' – a honey trap sent in to snare or even kill Nero. It was too much of a coincidence considering who he was.

***

Elvira walked through the door past an en-suite and built-in wardrobe either side and into the modest hotel room. She looked around, mentally taking notes of her surroundings, as was her habit. Large windows dominated the room, the curtains half shut, the hum of the carnival drifting up from the street. The double bed was made up with bedside tables and a wooden desk with the usual hotel paraphernalia on top.

"*Mi casa es su casa* – the drinks should be up soon. It's Ana, right?"

Elvira turned to him with a broad smile. "You forget already? Yes, it's Ana. Leon?" She had no doubt "Leon" was nowhere near his real name. He returned the smile, nodded and tossed his keycard onto the desk. Elvira slipped off her backpack and casually dropped it by the bed, running her other hand over the bedspread. "I do love good hotels. It's the little things like the soaps and shampoos in the bathroom, everything on call," she cooed.

"Not having to clean up after yourself?" he added with a wry smile.

She laughed and sat down on the side of the bed facing the window, gently bouncing on it as if testing the mattress.

"You don't stay in hotels much, then?" he asked, crouching down in front of the minibar before opening it up and peering inside.

"No," she sighed. "I am a budget traveller – hotels too expensive."

"Where are you staying?"

"Down near Parque San Telmo. I stay in Las Palmas for two or three days, then maybe travel to the other islands."

"You want a gin or something?" he asked, peering into the array of drinks in the room's minibar.

"Hmm, I wait for the bubbly stuff." She let out a long sigh and leaned back on the bed, spreading herself out.

He turned to glance at her and she gave him her most seductive look while patting the side of the bed. "Why don't you wait here?"

She was well aware she was no catwalk model but knew she had an undefined beauty that men always locked onto. Leon, or Tom as he wasn't revealing to her, stood up with a hint of galvanised lust in his eyes. He then moved across the room, glancing towards the door.

"Maybe we'd better wait—"

She let out a light giggle. "Of course, what kind of girl do you think I am?" The words came automatically, relayed so many times before. She was in the full flow of her act, a naïve travelling student, out for a good time, seeing some of the world before returning to "university in Latvia". Seduction was her speciality; she had been carefully trained in these matters. It should be straightforward: a few glasses of champagne when it arrived, give him a few tantalising glimpses of her body, a taste of her lips then retrieve her special powdered cigarettes from the bag when he was distracted. A secondary follow-up message to the Ghost Order had requested her to try and extract information by questioning, some torture techniques would almost certainly be required, then eliminate if necessary.

He stood next to her, running a hand through her dyed-blonde hair.

"Well, I had some thoughts on that."

There was a gentle tap at the door. "Room service," came an accented voice on the other side.

"Don't go anywhere," he said in a low murmur.

As the target went to the door, Elvira leaned over and quietly unzipped the pocket of her backpack. Scopolamine, the drug from Colombia that turned the hapless victim into a willing zombie accomplice. A few sprinkles of the odourless powder she had put in a few of the cigarettes should do the trick.

There was a pop as the champagne was corked at the door and a low murmur of conversation as "Leon" accepted the delivery.

"If you could just sign for it here, sir," she heard the hotel concierge say. She pulled out a small tablet canister and slipped it into her jeans front pocket, ready to administer, and placed the cigarettes on the side table.

"Thank you, that's very generous," the concierge said.

Nero returned to the room holding a silver tray, ice bucket with the bottle and placed it down on the desk, his back to her. She heard the fizz as the liquid hit the glass and he handed her one and held up his.

"Well, *salud*, Miss Ana." She took a sip as he gulped down a mouthful and let out a satisfied sigh. "Not bad stuff. Certainly not the first drink or the last—"

She placed her glass on the bedside table, picked up the Donskoy cigarettes and offered one to him. "You want?"

"No, I'm good, but you go ahead."

She nodded, keeping her expression unreadable and slowly took out a cigarette, then played with it, unlit, between her fingers. She would need to get the powder from the tablet canister into his drink or think of something else.

He sat down on the edge of the bed next to her, his eyes furtively checking her out, then he held up the glass again as if to toast.

"To – what's the next island you're visiting?"

She picked up the glass again and clinked his.

"Lanzarote or Arrecife, I'm not sure."

"Here's to Lanzarote or 'not sure,'" he repeated with a smile.

"So, how does this carnival compare to others, Ana?"

She shook her head, a dull pain now penetrating her skull.

"No, I haven't been to many other carnivals. Las Palmas is my...first." She felt sick for a moment, drowsy.

"Maybe Rio would be worth putting on your itinerary, Ana?"

She ignored his words, trying to move to the far side of the bed. Something was wrong.

"Ana isn't your real name, is it? But then I'm no Leon," he said with a light chuckle.

She had screwed up, had been so fixated on getting him drugged that she had let her guard down. Her vision blacked out, the dizziness coming over her in waves, a cold sweat soaking her skin and her heart seemed to be pounding through her chest.

Fuck!

It was her last thought as she fell onto the floor, a void of blackness tunnelling her vision.

***

Frank had intercepted the concierge as he made his way through the long hallways of the ground floor of the hotel with the champagne for room 207. After dragging him into one of the restrooms he had knocked him out and thrown on his jacket and name badge. Next, he took a small package from his backpack supplied by Rhodes and prepared a small sample of benzodiazepines, a central nervous system depressant in the form of tablets. Between his thumb and forefinger, Frank crushed one up into one of the champagne glasses.

Then he took a pen from the concierge's jacket and scribbled a note in clear capital letters on the order pad with the introduction code he was to give Nero on their first meeting alerting him to who Frank was, along with a warning that his visitor in his room was an immediate threat.

There could be no misunderstanding although there were undoubtedly multiple things that could go wrong. What if the woman answered the door instead of him?

He'd have to deal with that problem if it came up. There was no time to think or plan and this was the best idea considering his resources.

Frank wheeled the trolley up to the elevator and headed up to the second floor, then continued to the room. Only a hotel guest passed by, barely glancing at him.

It was a big relief to see Nero open the door. Frank immediately held up the note along with a finger over his lips. Nero read it, frowning, then looked at Frank and nodded.

He understood.

"Good evening, sir. Your ordered beverage," Frank said in an accent. He gestured with a hand sign to one of the glasses, then pointed past the guest's shoulder into the room and made a sipping motion with his hand.

"If you'd just sign for the order, I'll open the bottle for you," Frank continued and did so with a loud "pop" and placed it back into the ice bucket.

He jabbed his finger again at the same glass, emphasising to use the correct one. Nero nodded again and gave a thumbs up.

"Thank you, sir, that's very generous," Frank said, before pointing at the floor to indicate he would wait.

Nero took the tray and stepped back inside. Frank waited outside, glancing up and down the corridor, ready to look busy with the notepad if anyone passed by.

After barely a few minutes the door opened, and Nero gestured him inside. Frank shut the door and walked in to see the woman lying on the floor, out cold.

"Did she bring a bag?" he asked. Nero pointed a finger at the far side of the bed. Frank picked it up and unzipped it before tossing out the contents: bottled water, a spare zip-up jacket and a small toolkit containing pliers but little else.

Frank held it up for Nero to see. "Not sure what she was gonna do with these, use them on your balls, maybe?" Frank said, grinning. His new acquaintance didn't smile back and glanced down at the girl again, forlornly.

Frank looked into the now-empty bag.

"Well, no phone, ID or anything that hints at her identity – help me get her back on the bed."

They placed the unconscious body on top of the bedspread.

"Are you sure she's some kind of agent?"

"I don't know what she was planning, but something wasn't right..." Frank began as he searched her jeans pocket. He immediately found the small pill capsule bottle and held them up, "Drugging you by the looks of it. Probably not to take advantage of you either." He pocketed the bottle and glanced at the Donskoy cigarette packet.

"Did she offer you a cigarette?"

"She did."

"They're probably drugged too. We'll take them with us."

Frank turned to Nero who was standing cross-armed, still looking stunned.

"So what do I call you – Nero?"

The young man shook his head, "Mark Simpson is fine," he said, holding out his hand.

"I'm Frank," he replied, shaking it.

"Alright, Frank. Thanks, by the way. Didn't think we'd meet like this."

"I take it you booked into the hotel under Mark Simpson?"

Nero looked regretful. "Yeah, yeah I did."

"OK, not ideal but maybe it won't matter. We should be off the island in a matter of hours." He glanced back at the woman. "She should be out for an hour at least, a couple at most. We need to leave ASAP."

"What about her?"

Frank glanced around the room. "Well, there's nothing we can tie her up with unless you've got something?"

"Like ropes?" Mark shook his head. "No, buddy."

"Best we can do is lock her in then, cut the phone line and take her stuff. Let's get started."

Chapter 13

Early the next morning Frank made his way to La Luz Port and took a while looking for the ship *Anita*. It was hard to miss; a colossal beast, the dark hull casting welcome shade across the dock. From the bridge to the bow, towering lift rigs hauled the deck containers into bays, stacking them into blocks that reminded Frank of the toy Lego bricks Joe used to love playing with. Straddle-carriers brought a constant stream of containers for loading. He watched the process for a while, keeping his eyes along the dock and sat down.

They had slipped out of the hotel and holed up at Frank's apartment for a few hours, then left individually and made their way to the dock. Frank messaged Rhodes with news of the 'new player in the game'. Rhodes had told him to stick to the plan. Frank didn't like it. Things were already going south, and they hadn't even left yet.

Ten minutes later, the figure of Nero appeared, looking every bit like a backpacker. He glanced in Frank's direction for a second but didn't acknowledge him and began to climb up the passenger gangway. Frank checked his watch. There were two and a half hours before the ship was due to leave but Frank was wary of hanging around too long. He got up, grabbed his bag and walked over to the gangway entrance. A squat, bearded crewman greeted him who mumbled something that Frank barely heard as he tried to get past the man.

"Ticket?" The man asked again, slightly louder in a heavy accent.

"Oh sorry, mate." Frank handed him the paper folder that Rhodes had given him. The crewman checked the details and gave him a friendly grin. "We don't have too many passengers. It's very rare."

"Well, I just hope I don't cause the ship to sink," Frank replied. The crewman laughed and held out his hand. "My name is Yuri, I'm the first mate on the ship, and I welcome you to the *Anita*."

Frank was shown to his quarters, deep in the belly of the ship. The crewman gave him a rapid rundown of the schedule, mealtimes and so forth and promised he would check in with him later that evening. It was surprisingly comfortable and clean, almost like a basic cruise cabin. He slumped his backpack down, took a shower and changed clothes, giving himself a short time to rest. He almost drifted off but was pulled back into consciousness by the ship's horn blasting from above. He peered out of the porthole as the dockside began to pass by slowly. They were setting sail.

He moved down the corridors, passing crew cabins to find his way up top to the deck. In the passageway exposed pipes laced the ceiling overhead, interspersed with thick hatch doors. After taking a few flights of metal steps, Frank came to an exterior door and stepped out onto the main deck, at the mid-section of the ship. He glanced back at the bridge castle, a white block structure dotted with a row of tiny windows where, Frank guessed, the captain spent most of his time. He strolled towards it, getting a feel for his bearings, passing the lifeboats before eventually coming to the stern behind the bridge.

A crewman dressed in a blue boiler suit walked by and nodded a silent greeting but, other than that, the ship seemed ghostly quiet. Then Frank saw Nero, leaning over the railings at the back of the boat, watching the port of Las Palmas shrink on the flat sea.

He leaned over next to him. "Goodbye, Las Palmas," Frank said. The younger man turned, appraising Frank with a glance, smiled and turned back to the view.

"Yeah indeed. I'll miss the sand sculptures. Any sign of our friend?"

"No, it seems clear. I'm just glad we're on our way," Frank replied. "Just so you know, I'm travelling under the name of Frank Milligan," he added.

"Milligan? Did you choose that name or was it given to you?"

"What difference does it make? We can swap real names later. Eaglecraft wants you at his RZ without any hiccups. So I hope we get along as it might be a long journey, mate."

Nero gave a quiet snort of derision. "Eaglecraft, nice. Assume he picked that one himself," Nero stood up straight, turning to Frank. "Why we couldn't just fly, I'll never know?"

"Did he not explain to you?" asked Frank with mild irritation. "It's longer but far more secure. Less airport security, a lot more under the radar."

"Sure," Nero said with finality.

"What cabin are you in?"

Nero sighed, "134."

"Alright. I'm just down the corridor: 102. We need to remember these things, just in case."

The young man nodded. "Yes, I understand...Mr Milligan."

"Good. Well, I'm gonna take a look around the ship. I'll catch you later."

The younger man nodded and returned his gaze to the port disappearing on the horizon.

Chapter 14

Elvira drifted back into consciousness with a sour taste in her mouth and a pounding headache. Before she even opened her eyes, she knew something was wrong. A deep feeling of unease had settled on her and on seeing the hotel room it all came back.

Shit!

She had fucked up and, worst of all, she had been played. Stupid!

With waves of nausea washing over her, she forced herself to sit up on the bed and glanced down to where her backpack had been. It was long gone. Luckily she hadn't anything in the bag that could compromise her, but it was still bad news. She glanced at the ice bucket and bottle neck sticking out in disgust with herself. The glasses were gone, naturally.

You're still alive, Iskra. Next time you won't be so lucky.

She patted her jeans pocket and knew that the tablet canister with the Scopolamine had been taken, then went to the bathroom, splashed cold water over her face and proceeded to search the room, just in case. Finding nothing, she slipped out and down to the lobby. The party crowds had long dispersed, but a policeman was speaking to one of the reception staff and a dishevelled concierge. She walked past and loitered by a table of newspapers just within earshot, pretending to read the headlines.

There were snippets of conversation in Spanish – the concierge had been knocked out by someone – no, he didn't see who it was; he was just on his way to deliver drinks to room 207. A Mr Simpson.

The policeman asked to see the room and at that Elvira left through the doors into the morning sun.

So, an imposter concierge that came with the drinks, the one she had not seen. Nero had help, that much was now certain. She tried to analyse why she had not been more alert, but all the intelligence had led her to believe he was an office boy without external help.

Not so.

She would report that, but not yet. She needed some lead as to why the seemingly straightforward objective had not been completed.

The target and his new accomplice would be leaving the island, somewhere. She had to find them.

Chapter 15

Frank headed below deck, past the lower stowage holds and along a walkway that ran alongside the crates in the lower 'tween decks. He came to a blue sign that labelled the decks alphabetically and looked for the mess hall where he could get a bite to eat. After negotiating another labyrinth of corridors and hatches, Frank came to a large room with several round tables, all immaculately laid out ready for the evening meal. A board on the wall displayed a menu which Frank studied before a cook's mate walked past.

"Hello," he chirped.

"Hi, I don't suppose I can grab a snack, like a sandwich or something? I haven't eaten for a while," Frank asked politely.

"No problem. I can fix you something. What would you like?"

"Anything: ham, cheese, I'm not fussy."

The cook nodded and disappeared through the metal door off the mess. After ten minutes he returned with a steak and onion sandwich on rye bread with a small side salad.

"Ah, you're a star. Thanks, mate."

The cook grinned. "My pleasure, let me know if you need anything else," he said as he returned to the kitchen.

A tall man with a shaved head and tattoos on his neck and arms entered the mess, glanced over at Frank, smiled and disappeared into the kitchen. Frank chewed his food, staring out across the vast ocean.

After five minutes he heard a voice and looked to see the same man walking up to the table holding a plate and steak sandwich.

"I saw yours. It looked so good I thought I'd join you."

Frank smiled politely, but he wanted to be alone with his thoughts.

"Hi. No problem," Frank heard himself say.

The man sat down and extended a large hand.

"I'm Lukas. Second mate of the *Anita*." Frank detected a slight accent. Slavic, perhaps.

Frank shook it. "Frank Milligan, nomad of the seas."

Lukas laughed.

"So, how long have you been a seaman?" Frank asked.

"Over ten years. I was in the Russian navy before."

Frank paused for a moment before eating the last of his late lunch. A memory reared its ugly head: the Russian mob he had come up against less than a year before.

"I assume Russia is your home then?"

"Yes. St Petersburg. What brings you on the *Anita*? You're travelling?" the Russian asked.

Frank wiped his mouth with a paper napkin and leaned back, gazing back out of the window.

"Yes, a bit of a life change. Get away from England for a while."

"That's great. I'm very jealous. For me, life is just hard work. But I have a plan. I save my money and hope to make sailing trips around Panama and Colombia."

"Sounds like a nice plan," said Frank with genuine interest. Sailing had been a hobby he'd always promised himself but never got around to. Perhaps after this job.

Lukas finished his sandwich and stood up.

"Sorry, I have to go. Do you play Poker, Frank? The crew sometimes have a game – if you want to join?"

Frank held up a hand. "I'm fine, thanks for the offer."

"Alright, well, if you change your mind. The captain even likes to play on occasion."

Frank smiled as Lukas walked off.

"I'll bear that in mind, thanks."

Frank was wary. A reminder that although they might be heading to the middle of the Atlantic, he needed to stay alert. If they had tracked Nero to Las Palmas was it such a wild notion that they had people on the ship? Frank silently cursed Rhodes for not changing their route.

Chapter 16

Mid-Atlantic. Five days later.

The days and nights had merged into one, drifting by like the ship's journey across the vast expanse of the endless ocean surrounding them. Occasionally other ships appeared, mere specks in the far distance and the sunsets seemed to become more spectacular the closer they came to the Caribbean. Frank was surprised at how calm the crossing had been. There had been one or two rough nights but, overall, it was a case of getting used to the rolling movement and adapting to it. The wonder of the natural order of things certainly put things into perspective for Frank.

Frank and Nero were invited to the Officers' Recreation room to enjoy an aperitif before sharing another excellent dinner with the captain. The ship was due to dock at Antigua the following day. Captain Nicolae Petrescu was from Romania, a tall man with a typically rugged demeanour who seemed to enjoy the small talk with his only two passengers. They would be there for a few days, unloading around twenty containers, so the captain suggested Frank take a trip around the island. The rest of the officers hailed from Lithuania, Georgia and Bulgaria. The two passengers recited their stories, keeping to the script of their legends as the captain drained his wine glass.

"The crew sometimes have a game of Poker. Would you care to join us?"

Nero shook his head immediately. "I'm gonna have an early night, don't feel too great, so I'll pass."

The captain smiled politely. "No problem, Mark." His gaze turned to Frank who felt like wheeling out a similar response. Still, perhaps it wouldn't be a bad idea to bond with the crew and captain.

"Sure, I'll try a few hands. Your first mate mentioned it – Lukas?"

The captain chuckled. "Ah yes. He already asked you? No surprise. He is an excellent player. You watch him carefully."

***

A few of the crewman, including Lukas, the captain and Yuri sat around a small table in the mess, cards and chips scattered across the table. Lukas put down shot glasses and a bottle of vodka. Frank groaned inwardly and shook his head.

"It's a ship tradition. Come on." The captain poured the clear liquid and put Frank's shot in front of him with a slam.

"Alright," Frank muttered reluctantly. He picked up his glass and toasted the captain's health.

Frank began his game well, winning a hand with style before the luck – and the money – began running dry. It seemed the other players always had one slightly better hand than him and their bluffs were top notch.

On throwing down his hand and once again declaring he was out of the game, Lukas began to push some chips over the table.

"Here. Have these—"

Frank shook his head. "No, Lukas, keep them. I should call it a night."

A brief expression of offence passed across the Russian's face, and he shoved the chips in front of Frank anyway, then nodded with finality and pointed at Frank's hand of cards face down on the table.

"You play – and drink."

Frank couldn't help but laugh out loud as he picked up his cards. There was no avoiding the directness of the Russian. Frank was beginning to feel at home with the crew.

After a few hours, just the captain, Lukas and Frank were left at the table, on top a scattering of cards, several empty bottles and a full ashtray. The men had stopped playing.

Frank slammed down his shot glass, having learned it to be the standard protocol and leaned over toward Lukas.

"You're not bad for a Russian," he murmured.

Lukas laughed. "Sounds like you had a bad experience with my countrymen, Frank."

"Yeah, you could say that—" He was thinking of the thugs who had kidnapped his wife and kid again. He shook his head and waved away the thoughts. "I'm stereotyping, sorry."

Nicolae, the captain, held up his hand. "Frank, don't apologise. I hate the Russians too." They all laughed.

There was a moment of silence.

"You have family, Frank?"

He nodded automatically, aware he was being unguarded but past caring. "I do, and hopefully they're tucked up at home, safe."

"So, you travel and leave them behind," said the captain. He quickly held up his palm. "I'm not judging; we all have to do what we do," he said, plainly. Both men looked at Frank as if understanding something unsaid. As if they knew who he really was.

Lukas stood up. "I'm done. Early shift tomorrow—" He slapped Frank on the shoulder.

"I think we're all done," smiled the captain, raising his glass at Frank before draining it.

***

The next morning, feeling worse for wear and still reeling from his bad run at the Poker, Frank checked on Nero, banging loudly on his door.

"Yeah? What is it?" Nero shouted.

"Just checking you're in there."

"Thanks. Yeah, I'm still here," came the unimpressed reply. Frank went to the canteen and grabbed a coffee before heading up on deck to watch the island of Antigua come into view. A deep blue sky stretched unending overhead, and gulls circled the ship as it slowly approached St John's Port.

Once docked, Frank leaned over a rail sipping the coffee, watching the activity below as local dockworkers secured the boat, followed by a few crew members from the *Anita* spilling onto the scorched concrete dockside from the ship's hull.

After a few minutes, a group of three travellers moved forward to board. Another two men, one with slick black hair, the other with a reddish crop, both in short-sleeved shirts and long shorts loitered farther back. They both cast their eyes up over the ship, their suitcases at their feet before pulling them toward the gangway. The crewman checked the traveller's tickets and let them on board. Frank appeared to watch the dockside gantry crane unloading the containers, but his attention focused on the two men.

Chapter 17

Frank hadn't bothered taking a trip around the island. It felt like he should stay on board, stay alert and keep an eye on Nero, who had taken ill. Something was spiking in his senses, and he wanted to follow his own lead. The ship set sail around 6.30PM and a half-hour later Frank rapped on Nero's door. "You eating?"

There was a pause followed by a light groan. He knocked again. "Mark?"

"I'm going to skip the dinner. Still feel like shit. You go ahead."

"Alright. I'll be back in an hour."

Frank walked up the stairs to the lower decks, looked up and down the empty corridor and then descended, lurching into the side of the stair rail from a roll of the ship. The weather seemed to be getting more stormy. When he went to the canteen, it was empty. No one around, not even the cook.

Frank opted for a sandwich and a plastic bottle of water from the vending machine. The big lunch he had indulged in still weighed on his stomach. He paused at one of the tables about to sit down, then thought better of it and headed back to the cabins.

When he arrived, he unlocked his door and was about to step inside but noticed Nero's door ajar further down the corridor. He quickly put his food and drink down and walked up to the door, then stopped and listened carefully.

Slowly, he pushed the door further ajar and looked into an empty cabin. He walked inside, "Mark?"

No answer.

Frank checked the en-suite bathroom. Wet towels were sprawled all over the floor, his wash bag was still there, and in the main cabin, his backpack and clothes were scattered over the bed.

He was gone.

Frank rushed down the corridor in the opposite direction from the canteen. The first thing to do was alert the captain and take it from there. He couldn't have got very far, thought Frank. We're on a ship, for God's sake.

Frank decided to check outside first. Nero sometimes went out there for a cigarette. He ran up the stairwells of the midship, up past the second and third decks and came to a hatch for outside.

The wind pressed against him like an unseen hand as he stepped through and he had to push hard on the door to fully open it. Outside the sun had long gone, plunging the ship into darkness apart from the sporadic deck lights. At the bridge castle, he saw figures through the windows. It seemed busy up there. He walked in that direction, looking across the cargo hatch covers to the other side, then noticed a figure at the bottom of the steps to the bridge. Nero or one of the crew? Frank couldn't quite make them out, but it looked like they were standing guard from their posture.

In the distant darkening sky there was a tiny flashing light from a plane. As he moved along the deck, there was movement in the bridge window, silhouettes across the stark light. Someone was shoving one of the crew, and he swore he saw the outline of a gun.

Frank stopped and slid into a dark alcove.

Something's up.

Nero was missing. New faces had just boarded. Frank's instinct was on full alert, and he didn't need to convince himself there was a situation developing here.

He moved stealthily along the deck, half crouched toward the figure at the bottom of the steps, now guarding access to the bridge. It looked like a crew member from the jumpsuit he wore, but the black greased back hair didn't look familiar. As the man glanced in his direction his face was clearly lit by one of the exterior lights – one of the new passengers he had seen on the dockside who had boarded at St John's. He had a handgun in his hand, casually holding it down by his side.

Frank stood there, frozen in the shadows, watching. He couldn't tackle the man from the front, there was too much distance, and the greaseball would easily have time to get a shot off. Frank reached into his pocket and pulled out a coin. He tossed it onto the deck the far side of the man with a metallic clank. The man turned to face the noise, his pistol rising, pointing at the unknown.

As soon as his back was turned, Frank moved forward in a half-crouch towards his assailant. When he reached him, Frank's left arm swiftly moved around the man's neck, dragging him back and off balance. He grabbed the arm with the weapon and yanked back hard. Greaseball's arms hyper-extended, his elbow pivoting on Frank's chest, the gun falling away from his grip.

As they stumbled backwards, Frank slipped, losing his grip on the arm and his assailant. Instinctively, he planted his feet for better grip on the deck, recovering his footing. Then, a jolt of pain across his face. Greaseball had thrown his head backwards, connecting squarely with Frank's nose. Eyes watering, he turned away. Immediately, a barrage of punches came raining in. Hands came up fast to block, but one connected with Frank's temple with a dull thud. His legs collapsed beneath him, sending him sprawling on the hard decking.

Frank was dazed, but he curled up into the foetal position, waiting for the world to stop turning. As the inevitable rain of kicks came in at him, Frank braced, many of the blows on his arms and legs.

Through one eye, Frank saw Greaseball raise his foot, about to stamp on his head. He rolled quickly, grabbing the assailant's supporting leg and driving all his weight through it.

Greaseball flipped backwards, his head bouncing off the deck.

Frank leapt up, sitting on top of him in a securing mount. Then he rained punches down with dull thumps, focusing all his hatred on that face until the assailant was out cold, his face bruised and broken like a beetroot on a bad day.

Frank crawled off the figure, breathing heavily and forced himself up onto his feet. He looked around and found the weapon, a Glock 13 near the bottom of the bridge steps, and checked the chamber.

All good, now he had a piece.

He pulled the unconscious guard down the deck to the lifeboat area and into a hidden nook then headed back, creeping up the bridge steps, the barrel of the Glock aimed straight ahead. The ship rolled as if a storm was rising. A buzzing that Frank only just became aware of grew louder.

There was a change in the light, in the pattern of shadows. Overhead, a helicopter suddenly came into view, a spotlight shining down onto the far side of the bridge castle. A figure in black appeared in the door and dropped down a line, before proceeding to fast rope down onto the deck. From his position, Frank could see another person appear at the helicopter door holding some sniper rifle. It was hard to make out, but Frank swore it was the woman they'd encountered in Las Palmas.

With a scurry of footsteps, Frank came to the bridge door. For the first time, he saw the situation inside. Nero, hands seemingly tied behind his back, was being held at gunpoint by another man, one of the recent embarked. Nicolae, the captain, was navigating the ship with a grim expression, evidently forced to carry out the gunman's bidding. The far exterior door opened and the masked abseiler entered, with a submachine gun at the ready and spoke a few words that Frank couldn't hear to his comrade.

Frank also realised for the first time that the ship had slowed right down to a crawl. The helicopter was now hovering to position itself in front of the bridge as if to land on the cargo bay.

They were taking Nero off the bloody ship.

Two targets and two friendlies inside the bridge. Too dangerous to go in shooting. All Frank could do was mix it up. It would alert them inside the bridge, but he had no choice. He moved back down the steps to a different position and got the helicopter in his sights and squeezed off a series of rounds aiming at the spotlight on the chopper.

The pilot, realising he was under attack, veered away quickly, the lights disappearing into the windswept darkness.

Frank moved back up the steps and glanced through the bridge-door window. The tall man with red hair that Frank had seen board earlier had a weapon to Nero's head and was pulling him out of the door on the far side, alerted by the shooting. The new arrival killed the lights inside the bridge, then began firing at the door Frank was behind, shattering the window. Frank took cover and heard the rush of footsteps on the far steps. He gingerly stood up and glanced through, where Nicolae had crouched down on the floor to hide. The others were gone.

"Nicolae!" Frank hissed. "Lock the doors! Quickly!"

The captain didn't hesitate to get back up and locked the far door, then rushed over to Frank.

"Who the hell are they?" he demanded.

"Don't know yet – barricade this the best you can, I'll be back."

Frank rushed down the steps quickly and jogged all the way around the back of the bridge tower, the massive ship funnel looming overhead. Stepping around the mooring gear, Frank kept close to the walls until he came to the other side and caught sight of the figures moving along the deck.

The helicopter was closing in again.

The only option was to cut off the assailant's escape.

First, he fired above the heads of the figures to get them to take cover.

Frank moved his aim at the dark shape of the chopper with both hands and continued firing, aiming more or less at the tank. *Pok! Pok! Pok!*

Then a flash of a muzzle from the 'copter door and a bullet hit a metal capstan drum right next to him with a pop.

The chopper billowed slightly, the bullets finding their mark. It swayed to the side and veered away from the ship, the side lights revealing a small column of smoke. Hopefully he'd done enough. Frank knew that despite how movies portrayed these events, tanks of fuel did not automatically explode when hit by bullets. It would have been nice if it had though, he thought.

On his haunches, Frank sensed the whizzing sound, followed by a close crack of metal hit near his body from the men on the deck. Time to move.

Frank duck-walked around a tube-like deck ventilator and kept his eye on them while the chopper now circled around the rear of the ship. The tone of the engine told Frank it was struggling, probably losing fuel fast. No doubt it had come from Antigua and could only now either land on the ship somehow or head home.

Now was the time to grab Nero. Frank stealthily moved up some steps to a walkway above where the assailants were. He half jogged a few metres, well away from the rails, so he was ahead of their position and lay low, peeping over to get eyes on them. Both assailants were heading in his direction, pushing at Nero and urging him forward as they scanned the dark sky. It seemed like they were desperately hoping the chopper would return to make their escape.

Frank slipped back out of sight, moving into the shadows. He heard them walk past, snippets of low whispers.

"Chopper went back. We're on our own"

"Fuckin' great. Where's the shooter gone?"

The abseiler jabbed a thumb over his shoulder. "Back there."

"Well, keep an eye on our six—"

The black figure of the abseiler dropped back and turned around to check his rear. Frank, crept forward, silently climbing over the railings.

The helicopter came into view above the containers that filled out the bulk of the ship, just for a few seconds then dived out of sight, the engine fading. It looked to Frank like they had aborted the mission and were leaving their buddies behind on the ship.

The abseiler came underneath Frank. He jumped down, just behind his footfall, driving his elbow into the back of his head with a well-aimed strike. The man stumbled forward, clearly dazed, there was a clunk as his gun hit the deck. Frank ran ahead, grabbing the abseiler around his neck. Pivoting, Frank turned to face Nero and the redhead who immediately raised his weapon.

Frank shrank back, using his hostage as a shield.

"Nowhere to go now your bird has gone. Give up, and I'll spare your life!" Frank shouted.

Red grabbed Nero by the collar, pressing his pistol into the base of his skull. Nero grimaced for a moment, staring at Frank, but his expression resolute.

"You want me to pull the trigger, buddy?" Red bellowed, "I'll happily splatter his brains across the deck right now. Let my associate go, then kneel down with your hands raised – you can go on your merry way, live your life."

"How stupid do you think I am?" countered Frank, "If you wanted him dead why go through all this bullshit trying to grab him? No, obviously want him alive, which means your threat is empty." Frank edged forward. "Now let him go and put your weapon down."

Red began backing off, slowly dragging Nero around the corner and out of view.

Frank almost didn't see it. A glint of a blade in the abseiler's hand.

The knife came at Frank's head, over his shoulder.

Instinctively Frank ducked down, the knife barely missing him. Not waiting for a second, Frank drove both of his knees into the back of his attacker's legs, pulling him backwards at the same time. As they fell, Frank rolled him, smashing his body onto the deck, face down ending up on top of him. Frank postured up, now straddling his attacker, and unloaded a continual assault of blows. Two connected with his cheekbone and Frank felt the abseiler stop struggling.

He pulled himself to his feet, plucked the knife from his hand and tucked it into his belt. He then dragged the barely conscious abseiler to the railings and hauled him overboard.

No time to fuck around.

He didn't want that one coming back into the game.

Frank was already moving down the deck as the body of his assailant hit the dark water with a massive splash.

Frank unclipped the magazine in his pistol to check his rounds, three bullets left, and then slammed it back in.

From what he could hear and see, the helicopter was long gone.

He made a quick assessment. Two assailants had been taken out by his own hand. Now there was just one he knew of with Nero. Could it have been a small infiltration team? The bigger questions of who they were would have to wait. Where had all the original crew gone? He had hardly seen anyone. Should he go back to the captain for more information? But Nero was the priority. He was supposed to have protected the asset, and now the poor bastard was being dragged around at gunpoint.

Got to sort this.

He moved fast, sprinting along the deck to catch up in the direction of the bow and almost stumbled into a body lying seemingly unconscious. He recognised the shaven head: Lukas.

He was lying half through the doorway of a hatch that was banging against his body with the rise and fall of the ship. Frank crouched over him and felt for his pulse. The poor guy was dead. Put up a fight and died for it. Frank didn't feel so sorry for putting abseiler guy overboard now.

Frank glanced through the porthole – the steps inside leading down into one of the cargo bays appeared empty. Squatting low, he opened it wider and listened. A shuffle of a footfall from the depths below.

Frank froze and narrowed his eyes, trying to make out something from the dark void. He moved slowly inside, descending one step at a time until he came to a walkway. Ahead, a mass of containers in an area the size of a football field. The black clouds moved through the gaps above.

A shot rang out and sparked off nearby metal. He crouched down quickly, locating the flash from the weapon from the centre of the containers.

Frank moved quicker, running down another set of steps until he was on the ground level of the bay and followed a narrow gap between the steel containers that towered high above like skyscrapers. Knowing they were twenty or so metres away, he moved quickly to close in. Above, a gap in the clouds revealed a half moon, bathing the containers in a soft light. Shadows shifted across the grid-like boxes, and Frank slowed down, inching around each corner.

He stopped and listened for any sounds that might give him a clue as to their position. His assailant was a professional and would have moved fast after firing.

Frank moved forward again, pieing the corners at each small cross-section where the bottom of the containers met. There was hardly any light in the deep bowels of the boat making Frank hesitant about moving forward.

It was like hunting blind.

A distant footfall echoed through the container corridors at the far end, toward the bridge tower at the back of the boat. Frank stalked the sound, step by step, then saw the figures climbing laddered rails that led to a higher walkway on the edge of the bay. Frank stealthily moved through the gaps until he had a more precise shot of the silhouettes which were now running overhead. He aimed at the figure, but just then Nero slowed as if trying to buy time. They were too close together. Then Red gave Nero a shove in the back, almost sending him sprawling before turning and firing a shot in Frank's direction. Frank ducked and began climbing up the ladder after them.

As he reached the top, Frank noticed the ship was turning around. The captain, now no longer under duress, must be trying to get back to St John's. That also meant he'd alert the authorities if he hadn't already, and serious questions would be asked. Frank slowed down, spotting them at one of the lifeboats at the bottom of the bridge tower. Red was making Nero prep the boat by pulling the levers to ready it for release to the writhing sea below.

Frank ducked into an alcove, trying to get a clear shot but Nero was in the way. Frank inched forward, keeping a straight aim in case a shooting opportunity arose. The assailant quickly turned, spotted him and fired off a shot, the bullet missing Frank by a whisker. He pressed in hard against a nook at the side of the walkway trying to figure out the best move.

Just then movement in his peripheral vision. Frank turned, but it was too late. What felt like a brick smacked into the side of his head. Frank hit the floor. It was Greaseball, standing over him wielding a bar.

Fuck. Should've dealt with him properly.

The man smiled down at him with evil menace through the bruises Frank had given him earlier and signalled his colleague, Red.

"Time you disappeared and let us get on with our job." He stepped forward, raised the steel bar, ready to swing it down on Frank's head. Already dizzy and reeling from the first blow, Frank gave an inward groan and then scissor-kicked the assailant's shin, trapping his ankles.

Greaseball grunted with pain just as Frank followed with a forward lunge, using his boot to kick his knee. There was a crack of bone followed by a shout of pain.

Frank grabbed the side of the railings and hauled himself up to his feet, the metallic taste of blood in his mouth. Throbbing pain shot through his skull. Greaseball recovered and somehow still clung to the bar, taking a final lunge at Frank with the last of his strength. Frank reacted with a sidestep, pivoted and pushed him, using his own momentum to send him over the railings. There was a cry of surprise. Then he disappeared into the inky ocean with a splash that quickly swallowed the bruised face. Whether he saved himself or drowned, Frank didn't care.

He refocused on Red who fired in Frank's direction again. Then the assailant shouted at Nero to get in the boat as he began to climb on board hesitantly. Frank dropped to his haunches and took a shot. Red spun around, his pistol dropping to the deck and slumped down to his knees. Frank moved in a scurry to reach him and kicked the weapon away, as Red remained on his knees, clutching his chest.

"Who are you?" Frank demanded.

The eyes looked up to him with resigned acceptability of death, and he smiled thinly.

"Who the hell sent you?" Frank repeated, with edgy impatience.

He slumped down onto his side, blood escaping his mouth as he began to bleed out, the pool expanding on the rusty metal floor. The eyes now staring sightlessly through the rails out to the black sea.

"Shit!" Frank shouted, then he stood up and went over to Nero and gestured for him to climb back out of the boat. He pulled off the gag from his mouth. Nero spluttered and swore.

"You alright, mate?"

"Alright? Sure, I'm having a great time." He looked down at the corpse near his feet. "I'm guessing you have no idea who they are?"

"No idea. Now, listen to me. The captain has turned around for Antigua. We need to be ready to get off this ship. The authorities will now get involved, and that's bad news all round."

Chapter 18

St John's, Antigua

The *Anita* docked once again at St John's just as dawn broke over the small town. Frank and Nero stood ready for a quick exit from the ship.

The captain had been a stoic type, apparently no stranger to the sight of bodies or blood. As these guys had held him at gunpoint while trying to kidnap his passengers he wasn't overly concerned about their fate. However he had tried to convince Frank to check in with the local police.

"I can't do that, Nicolae," Frank had said, "for reasons I can't tell you." Frank turned away and glanced towards the town, then added, "For what it's worth, I'm sorry those bastards killed Lukas." Frank genuinely felt in any other situation they might have become good friends.

The captain had sighed, accepting the situation, then nodded once, as if to say, "I'll take it from here."

Frank gave him a brief salute, shook his hand and then disappeared down the gangway with Nero onto the dock.

Frank hated leaving the captain in the lurch, a man he'd shared those vodka-fuelled poker games with, but what else could he do?

The captain could have chosen to dump the remaining bodies and say no more about it. Frank had offered to help him do that. The question remained: Who had those men worked for? The captain agreed to keep quiet for the initial few hours to give Frank and Nero a head start. "I knew you moved in dark waters, my friend," the captain had told Frank.

Through the sticky mid-afternoon heat they walked through the tourist spot around Heritage Quay, catering hard for the daily cruise ship passengers who invaded on a regular basis. Eventually they got away from the crowd, where the brightly painted houses hailing from a colonial-era changed to shanty timbered concrete block houses.

Behind St John's cathedral they found a roadside cafe with stickers in the window that promised an Internet connection. Inside, a television was showing a baseball game, and two older local men played cards in the corner while drinking the local stout. The Caribbean cafe owner, apron slung over his shoulder, greeted them both with a broad smile.

"You want some fine rum, gentleman? You look thirsty to me," he said with typical Caribbean joviality.

Frank gave an easy laugh and waved him off.

"That would be great some other time."

They ordered bottles of cold water, spicy rice and chicken lunch and took refuge under the cooling downdraft of the ceiling fan.

Frank took out his small laptop and, using the agreed security protocol, sent an encrypted message to Carl Paterson with a simple update:

'En route with baggage.'

He was deliberately vague. Frank had no idea how their location had been compromised. There was a terrible sense of déjà vu, and Frank wondered if he could go through all this again.

When it came to Rhodes, there was no other option but to leave a message. He asked for a pay phone, and the cafe owner showed him one around the back. Frank dialled the number, a South American message service. When the automated female's voice came on, he waited for the beep.

"This is Milligan calling, a message for Eaglecraft. I collected the baggage as requested but there's a problem with shipping. It appears the tax man wanted more duty and tried to intercept the package. Had to change plans and now we are using a different courier service. Will contact you when able. Hoping to avoid having to paying any more import duty."

He ended the call, yearned for some time to think and figure out who he could trust. But it was probably the case that they needed to keep moving, get off the island to mainland Central America.

Was it Carl playing some game? Would his old friend hang him out to be killed? Frank couldn't believe that. Was Rhodes specifically someone he could trust? He said all the right things. Certainly, he was anti-establishment and a dedicated believer in his cause. But that could also mean he had his own agenda, and Frank knew only too well how far men would go to advance their own purposes.

The food arrived, and they both tucked in without hesitation.

Nero appeared calm, despite his recent trauma.

"What's going on? You make contact with Eaglecraft, then?" he asked.

"It's all in hand. I'm sure it's just a blip," Frank replied, unconvinced.

Nero looked up at him.

"A fucking blip? That infil team was more than a blip!"

"I know that. Any ideas who they were?"

Nero shook his head and ate a mouthful of chicken. "No idea. One was American, so maybe CIA? But some of the others had accents."

Frank nodded.

"The helicopter might be a clue. It must have come back here somewhere. Our options are: keep running and hiding, but the helicopter might give us some clues about what we're up against – if we can find it. This is a small island and there's only one airport so my guess is if it's anywhere, it's there."

Nero threw down his fork angrily. "You want to go chasing ghosts? I'm far more concerned about reaching safety. Experiencing the 'safe'"

Nero made quote marks with his fingers, "'—passage' Eaglecraft promised so we do what we need to do. I'm not up for running about like a blue-assed fly around this island."

Frank simply raised his eyebrows at this outburst and calmly rounded up the last of the rice with his fork before replying.

"Listen, I understand your concern, mate. But while you're with me, we have to play by *my rules*. Okay? Besides, we'll have to head to the airport, anyway." He flashed Nero a sarcastic smile.

Chapter 19

Frank paid the bill and casually asked the cafe owner if he'd heard about a helicopter in trouble over the island. Unless it had crashed without anyone's knowledge, then the airport was the most logical place to try. The cafe owner then called them a cab.

As the taxi took them across toward V.C. Bird Airport, Frank got the same answer from the driver – a rumour about a helicopter trailing smoke as it flew – but not much else. They paid the driver and walked into the main building. It was a small airport, basic but functional. A group of three businessmen made their way out of the exit underneath large ceiling fans that made the temperature inside the building almost bearable. A large row of windows looked out across the single runway where heat shimmered off the Tarmac like a magician's illusion. A private jet took off running the full length of the runway to the edge of the coastline before climbing gracefully into the clear blue sky.

Frank headed for the departures ticket desks, while Nero took a seat and stared around at the small amount of airport activity. He asked what was available to South America, but the only flight running was to Panama City that evening. He booked two tickets under the identities Rhodes had given him and went back to Nero.

"We have our tickets and eight hours to kill," Frank said, looking around. "The steward said we could check in our bags early. Let's do that and find somewhere to keep out of sight. Then I might have a look around."

"All right, fine," said Nero, making it clear he didn't want to move anywhere.

With their bags checked in, they headed back out onto the road, walking back to a small hotel they had spotted on the way in. Then, slumping down on the most comfortable seats in the quiet bar they ordered a couple of cold beers. Frank gulped his down and stood up.

"You gonna stay here without getting grabbed this time?"

Nero slowly shook his head, his face impassive. "Don't worry, boss. Maybe you should leave me your weapon?"

"Nope," said Frank as he left the bar.

Frank walked back along the road, passing the main airport entrance again and continued until he reached a fence that separated the airstrip. There were several outbuildings built along the wall with mounds of earth and a few dormant diggers on either side. He continued walking past the last of the buildings and saw an inlet with two hangers inside the airport perimeter, where a small aircraft was visible in one of them. The other hangar had a steel-latticed pull-down door that hid the interior. From around the back of the plane came a figure of a maintenance worker. Frank stepped behind one of the concrete posts lining the fence and watched. The workman moved to the other hangar, pulled up the door a few feet and slid under inside.

Frank kept walking until he was at the end of the fence. Another large building marked the end of the airport where an eight-foot-high concrete wall stretched up to a pile of rocks. A loud roar passed overhead, and the incoming aircraft landed further up on the runway. Frank took a look around to check he was clear, jumped up and fluidly hauled himself over to the other side in a few swift moves. On the far side, he crouched, staying frozen for a moment, assessing the scene.

Across a stretch of open land that looked exposed were the hangars that appeared devoid of life. He looked back up the airfield towards the control tower, but the glinting dark glass told him little. There was a chance of being seen but how likely was it that busy controllers would stare out at this relatively quiet and distant corner?

Frank took a breath and walked casually toward the hangars as if he had every right to be there.

Goddamnit, don't get caught, it'll screw up everything.

He wondered if any of the assailants from the chopper were still around somewhere.

Got to be wary.

He reached the side of the first hangar. Now out of sight of the rest of the airport, he moved around behind the hangars and headed to the other side. As he came up to the shutter door, he heard some scraping noises. He crouched down and peeped round to look inside. There, on the back of a transport truck, stood a helicopter, almost certainly the one he'd encountered the night before. Black, with very few markings. A workman was busying himself at the back. Frank took out his pistol and slipped inside before hiding himself amongst a pile of boxes and engine parts. He waited for an opportune moment to edge closer to the chopper. Underneath and around the gas tank he could see the bullet holes that had come from his weapon.

A sudden sound of footfall from the rear of the hanger spiked his concentration, and he slipped back into the shadows as the young Caribbean approached. Frank needed information and decided to risk the potential consequences. When the young man walked by, Frank stepped out of his nook.

"Hey, buddy."

The young man turned with an expression of complete surprise.

"What tha hell—" His wide-eyed gaze went from Frank's face to his gun. Then he froze.

Frank held his Glock, steadily aiming the barrel at his chest and put a forefinger to his lips for a moment.

"Don't be afraid, I just need to ask a few questions," he said, reassuringly.

The man raised his hands unconsciously.

"Questions? Alright..."

"What's your name?"

"Vincent."

Frank jerked his head at the helicopter. "Alright, Vincent. This beast. Where'd it come from?"

"I−I don't know. It not normally based here. Some dudes come in it early yesterday. Tha's all I know, and that's the truth. I swear."

Frank nodded. It was unlikely he was lying.

"What'd they look like and how many?"

"Three men." Vincent then proceeded to describe the three Frank had encountered on the ship.

"Alright. I need to look inside, mate. Can you open the door? Remember, any quick moves or something I'm not expecting and my twitchy trigger finger will want to party, you understand?"

"You ain't gonna get no trouble from me, sir."

"Good. Open it."

Vincent proceeded to open the door and stood aside for Frank.

"Climb inside. The pilot seat. I don't want you running off." Vincent did as ordered and Frank started in the rear seats, running one hand down the side and underneath, looking for anything that might help him out. Nothing. Then he moved to the co-pilot seat and did the same. It had been cleaned thoroughly, and Frank knew there was nothing to be found here that could help him out.

"One last question − did you clean up the helicopter?"

The young guy nodded his head vigorously. "Yep! Vacuumed and scrubbed as ordered by the boss guy." He jerked a thumb over his shoulder towards the main airport building.

"Show me where you put the trash?"

The man looked at him, genuinely puzzled by this request and led Frank to the back of the hangar and gestured at a bin liner and the dormant vacuum.

"Jus' this...nuthin' but dust and shit."

Frank glanced to the main doors, then jerked his weapon at the vacuum.

"Just open it up. Let's see what's in there."

Another look but he obeyed and took out the bag from the vacuum and opened it up; thick wads of fluff and dust, as expected. Frank bent down and rummaged through it with his fingers and pulled out a cigarette butt; the brand still visible along the filter: Donskoy. The same brand the girl had smoked or at least partly laced, in Las Palmas, that packet now in his possession. Undoubtedly her on the helicopter. The question was: who was she working with?

***

Fifteen minutes later, Frank returned to the wall, climbed over and headed back to the hotel. He had led the man to the rear of the hangar and apologetically tied and gagged him after Vincent revealed his shift change was in a few hours. Then Frank slipped a fifty-dollar bill in his top chest pocket. He couldn't risk him raising the alarm before flying out of there.

He still needed to know what he was fighting against and who. The thought crossed his mind to update Carl but could he trust him? It seemed a stretch to suppose he had anything to do with all this. Even so.

No, he would leave Carl out of the loop, for now.

Back at the hotel, Nero was still waiting in the lobby bar, looking bored.

"I thought you took off. Find anything out?"

"Yeah, I found it in a hangar. Everyone else involved seems to be long gone. Hard to know. It looks like your date from Las Palmas was definitely on that chopper though.”

Nero looked aggrieved at the suggestion she was his date, but said nothing.

“I have to make a call,” Frank said and walked off to call Rhodes.

There was a booth near the small hotel entrance, and Frank watched as two elderly retirees shuffled out then, satisfied he was out of earshot from anyone, picked up the receiver and dialled the number.

It was the message service again.

“It’s Mr Milligan about our transport again. There was a rogue package. One of the couriers; a female with dyed-blonde hair. I’ll email more details, and I’ll call back when I can.”

After the call, they left the hotel and entered the main airport building, once again as separate passengers. Frank stayed wary, keeping an eye on the other passengers or anyone else milling around. It seemed to him danger was lurking around every corner.

Chapter 20

Their flight arrived at Tocumen International Airport in Panama City, and the two made their separate ways, according to protocol, passing through the endless hallways and immigration lines before meeting up just near the airport exit. At VC Airport, just before they left, Frank had found an area of wasteland and cleaned, then dismantled the handgun before burying it in the ground. He felt naked without a weapon but smuggling a pistol through airport security, no matter how lax, was too risky.

"What now?"

Frank looked around and gestured at the tourist information desk.

"We'll need a map."

They took seats in one of the numerous coffee bars, away from the main foot traffic and Frank opened up the map on the table.

His eyes went to the border region and the notorious Darien Gap, the 10,000-square-mile area between Panama and Colombia. Frank remembered his background briefing on the country. There were various reasons for a 60-mile gap in the Pan-American Highway in that region. The sheer natural barrier of a vast untamed rainforest made building a road very difficult, and combined with the political corruption that was rampant there was little chance of it happening anytime soon. Last but not least was the dangerous presence of narco drug gangs, FARC, the communist paramilitary force as well as right-wing guerrilla groups were all known to operate freely in the area.

No, best avoid that region by any means.

"We'll want to keep moving down the country towards the border."

"We have several options. Fly on from here. That's the most obvious – or we could disappear in Panama City for a while, take another way – a bus or something," Frank paused, gathering his thoughts. "I think we go to Albrook Airport for a plane to Puerto Obaldia. From there we can get a boat to Capurganá in Colombia. We need to keep away from major airports which means taking some longer routes. It's getting too dangerous now."

Nero looked resigned to some preordained fate for a moment, then nodded.

"Sure, buddy. And our friends? They still snappin' at our tails, you think?"

Frank looked around the airport at a constant stream of passengers walking towards the departure gates. "We have to be cautious. Keep your face down, away from cameras while we're here—"

Just then two armed policemen walked past. One looked in their direction. "Just look at the map," Frank whispered, and they both looked down. Nero pointed to an area on the map as if they were discussing plans. The cops seemed to take an age crossing the gap between the two pillars, both of them now actively scanning the cafe from behind mirrored sunglasses.

From Frank's peripheral vision he could see they were passing by before disappearing into the crowd.

"All right, panic stations over," Frank sighed.

He couldn't stop wondering who their pursuers were, who that blonde woman was? Had they lost them or were they being watched right now? The old uncertainty and twists of the game pulled at his stomach. All Frank and Nero could do was keep running, get to the RV.

"Let's get out of here," Frank said, folding up the map.

Nero insisted on buying a fresh pack of cigarettes before they made their way outside where Frank hailed a cab. The taxi snaked its way through the night traffic of Panama City and then dropped them off at Albrook Airport. A sea of faces greeted their gaze, backpackers, locals, entire families all filling the small terminal. While Nero got their tickets, Frank scanned the faces in the crowd for any sign of recognition from the previous flights and airports. A good surveillance set-up would rotate operatives, of course, but it was worth staying vigilant. His mind kept returning to wherever the hell this crew was from.

Got to get there. Keep this kid alive. Get the job done.

After an hour of waiting around, they walked out to the Panama Airways small, rotary-engined plane. When Frank got on board, he noted there were only twelve seats. He checked the faces of all the passengers, one by one. No recognition. Every person aboard was Latin American apart from them.

Frank hoped they served beer, he needed one, just to relax. It had been a testing few days but, to Frank's disappointment, there was no beverage service at all.

The propellers kicked into action and, within a few minutes, they were airborne, flying over the outskirts of Panama City, the relentless lush green vegetation rolling away below them. The flight was short and, just under an hour later, the wheels appeared back in place from under the wing ready for touchdown. For a moment Frank caught a glance of the Caribbean Sea sparkling in the distance, then it disappeared behind the hills of the jungle. Frank stared out of the window at a tiny village of Puerto Obaldia, in the Kuna Yala indigenous region of Panama, consisting of single and double-storey buildings in blocks with painted balconies. The plane skirted along the dusty runway and all he could see for a few minutes was a hut on the side of the airstrip and jungle.

Once the light craft had pulled to a halt, the passengers jumped out. The pilot handed out the luggage, and then each passenger walked off towards the immigration hut. There were only six passengers including Frank and Nero so by rights the queue should have gone down quickly, but this was a South American official bureaucratic chokepoint. Nothing would happen soon. Frank could see a few main streets of the town. Beyond it, the sea. On his other side were hills of jungle growth that rolled off into the distance. Frank immediately understood why this area was not accessible by land.

"Any idea when this boat goes?" Nero asked, lighting a cigarette.

"I have no idea. We'll have to ask once we get in there," Frank muttered, casting a stare to the front of the queue in the building. On that note, a passenger came out past them with his passport stamped.

After another five minutes they finally got to the Panamanian border guard, dressed in camos that were more akin to some special forces unit than border security detail. Frank noted his sidearm tucked into a holster on his belt, a SIG Sauer P226.

The man stared down at Frank's passport – his Milligan legend – and looked up at him for a moment. "You need photocopies. Two!" He stuck two fingers up, emphasising his point in a seemingly rude gesture.

Frank nodded, understanding, and fished them out of his wallet. Luckily he already been warned about this from the tourist desk and had had them both get copies of their passports before taking the plane.

The soldier slowly took them and placed them down on the table in front of him and took his time checking the details. Finally satisfied, he grabbed a stamp and pounded them like pieces of meat being tenderised before handing it back.

"Adios."

Finally free to get the boat, Frank and Nero began walking along the fence by the small runway that resembled a short strip of road. There was a shout from behind them. The soldier was at the door waving a piece of paper.

"You forgot something?" Nero asked Frank.

There was a moment when Frank felt his senses spike as if he knew something was about to happen. He'd experienced it before.

"Oh he wants me to take the paper, I thought that was for—" Frank began.

Just then a shot rang out from the trees behind them. Frank and Nero both instinctively hit the ground fast. There was a shout from the village as another volley of gunfire burst through the trees, raking the ground in front of them.

"Back to the hut, we're in the open here," Frank hissed. Both men took off at full speed towards the hut, keeping themselves low to create a small profile. At the cabin they could both see the body of the Panamanian guard on the ground. As more shots rang out, they dived on the floor. On their stomachs now, they both crawled forward; edging towards a slight indent in the ground that might give them a few inches of safety.

Frank risked a glance and saw a stream of men starting to move through the trees, heading in their direction. They moved with military precision, and now Frank realised this couldn't be a coincidence. No way.

They reached the hut, moving behind it, giving them some cover from the incoming fire. Ahead of them in the village, people scattered, heading for cover. Frank remembered the sidearm on the border guard, but it was right in the firing line.

Frank couldn't see a way out except for straight ahead into the town, using the immigration hut as protection for their backs. Before he could give Nero the signal to move, they heard a shout from behind.

"No te muevas!"

Frank didn't move as instructed. With a side glance, he could see olive green trousers and army boots come into view, an AK-47 barrel aiming at his head. Frank closed his eyes not wanting to imagine what lay ahead.

Chapter 21

There were six men that Frank could see. Three were behind them and three ahead, all armed. The paramilitary soldiers had considered blindfolding them but decided that would make their progress too slow. One soldier had searched the prisoners and taken their backpacks but, at Frank's insistence, left them with their cigarettes. Then the group slowly trekked up the snaking path that cut into the jungle.

Were these guerillas just in the area and decided to grab a few tourists? But then why just him and Nero? Unlikely. The coincidence was too great.

It seemed their attempt to avoid the radar had backfired spectacularly.

This squad of soldiers must have come here specifically to pick them both up. Initially, they both acted like scared tourists, begging to be let go or to pay them for their release. But all pleas were met with silence. Frank tried to listen in on any muttered conversations, but the guerillas were professional and kept interpersonal comms to a minimum.

The jungle grew thicker, a cluster of deep green foliage interspersed with long, spiralling palms towered overhead. The air was scented with a fresh, woody aroma combined with the occasional scent of Jasmine. A chorus of chirping crickets along with a light buzzing of insects and the occasional squawk of birds in the trees accompanied their journey.

Frank kept glancing at the direction of the sun, trying to get his bearings when he could see it through the canopy. It had been too many years since he had gone through basic training on navigating by the sun or stars, but now was the time to dig into the memory bank. He still had his watch and on spotting sun rays through the trees, subtly held it up so the hour hand pointed at the sun. The imaginary line sitting between the hour hand and the 12 o'clock mark marked out north to south, at least giving him a rough idea of their direction. Taking into consideration that they were still in the northern hemisphere and it was March, the sun would rise directly east, Frank concluded. So it appeared they were heading south-west. He also tried to mentally calculate the distance going by their rough speed and the time while keeping his eyes peeled for any opportunities. Right now they were surrounded, and any sudden moves would probably end their lives.

Finally, they stopped in a clearing and a soldier told them to sit down, so Frank and Nero took a seat leaning against a nearby rock.

"*Agua, Por Favor*," Frank asked. They had not had any water since the kidnapping.

The squad leader, a man who looked in his mid-forties, gestured to one of the young soldiers who turned and fetched a metal water flask, then came back and handed it to Frank. He took a few swigs and gave it to Nero.

"What are we gonna do?" Nero whispered.

Frank looked over at one guerilla as he set down a radio transmitter and attempted to make contact. Frank supposed that it probably wasn't far off the mark that they were contacting their paymasters regarding their newly acquired treasure.

"Not sure. Nothing we can do right now."

"Just figured you'd have a plan."

"I'll think of a plan. Not much to work with right now."

The radio man began to speak low in Spanish and Frank strained to listen, looking down at his boots as if lost in thought. He could only catch snippets of words: '*carga adquirida cero quinientas horas*': Cargo acquired: 0500 hours.

The other soldiers were talking amongst themselves quietly, glancing over at their prisoners. One caught Frank's eye as he looked up and grinned eerily with tobacco-stained teeth. Frank wasn't sure who they were, but he guessed it was the AUC; the right-wing paramilitary group he had read about. Recalling his background notes on Colombia, he knew the militia had its roots in the 1980s when militias were established by drug lords to combat rebel kidnappings and extortion. In April 1997 the AUC was formed through a merger, orchestrated by the ACCU, an organisation of local right-wing militias.

If these guys were AUC then it would go some way to explain their current circumstances. The CIA most likely funded these guys and they were doing a little house cleaning for their sponsors.

After only ten minutes' rest, the two prisoners were ordered back to their feet. The terrain was getting steeper. There were points at which the men had to crawl on hands and knees, gripping tree roots that protruded out from the muddy ground. The rank smell of sweat and sounds of heavy breathing filled the air. Odd shouts in Spanish punctuated the silence as they navigated the trail. The hill finally levelled out, and the front guard hand-signalled to stop. A camp lay in a clearing ahead, where a bamboo hut protruded out from behind a clump of trees. The soldier on point continued, and the group entered another clearing. There were three small huts in the treeline, simple wooden constructs with bamboo roofs, draped with camo nets.

On one side was a cage, set apart from the huts, also made from wood with a solid floor and handles on either side for carrying. Frank sighed, knowing it was for them. It had just about enough space for three people. The door lay open.

"*Dentro!*" demanded the commander, jerking his pistol at them.

Frank fixed him a look and started to complain. The commander stepped forward and gave him a shove in the back.

"Get inside!"

Frank slowly got down on his hands and knees and crawled into the confined space. Nero followed, struggling into the cage and fell on his side. The door was slammed closed by one of the soldiers who proceeded to lean down and attach a hefty padlock. He leered down at them both as he got back up and walked away pulling a pack of cigarettes out of his chest pocket. Frank hauled himself into a sitting position. Leaning back against the tightly knit bamboo bars, he took a good look over the cage itself. He could see straight away that it wasn't particularly well made. That gave him a glimmer of hope in what had been a grim few hours. Perhaps it was just meant for just temporary imprisonment.

A guard sat himself down almost opposite, outside one of the huts, rested his AK on his lap and proceeded to sharpen a knife on a stone, while occasionally glancing over at them.

"Well, things are just getting better," Nero muttered.

"Shuddup."

"We should've tried escaping earlier, while we had a pissant's chance."

Frank couldn't have agreed more, but Nero's sniping was irritating him. He tried to think. It seemed like their captors were waiting either for further instructions or for a rendezvous to occur. If Frank's suspicions were correct, they either could wait until the exchange for an opportunity or attempt to escape now. He suspected that after the exchange escape would be almost impossible and the dark fate ahead probably involved torture, death or – most likely – both.

Next, he focused on the snippets of radio chatter he'd heard. Could a handover be happening at 0500 in the morning? The door opened from the main communal hut and, judging by the uniform, a commander wearing mirrored sunglasses who he hadn't seen before came out, glanced over at them before stepping into one of the nearby huts.

Frank looked around the clearing. Easily big enough for a chopper to land. That was what they must be planning.

That made sense.

"We've got to get out of here," Nero said suddenly, breaking the silence. He was staring over at the hut the commander had just entered. "They gonna kill us, I'm sure of it."

"Maybe. But wouldn't they have done it already?"

Before Nero could reply, one of the soldiers came over with a small plastic bottle of water and shoved it through a gap in the bars, with cooked rice wrapped in a dirty plastic carrier bag.

"Enjoy," he said in English and laughed.

"How long are you going to keep us here?" Frank asked with disdain.

"Maybe years for you," he said, with a smirk before walking off.

Nero ate some mouthfuls with his hands and handed it to Frank.

***

Darkness fell fast. Members of the guerrilla squad kept their camp mainly unlit, apart from inside one or two of the huts. Most of the men had gathered inside and, judging by the shouts and groans, it sounded like they were playing cards. Another soldier had come onto watch and sat opposite them, mainly smoking.

When he sensed the guard was distracted, Frank pressed the soles of his boots against the far side, testing for weaknesses. It was tied well and barely had any give. It would be pretty hard to kick through without a considerable amount of noise. His hands fell on the floor that had planked strips nailed to the structure.

Nero lay on his side in a foetal position.

"How did they bloody well find us?" The question came out of the blue. He tried to think back since the ship. It was possible they were tracked by someone at Antigua airport. Maybe seen at Panama airport through the security surveillance. If it had been when they had arrived in Panama, perhaps seen or picked up by a camera. Had Nero been flagged on facial recognition, or had their watchers just got lucky?

Then who had the power to then order a group of paramilitaries into position within an hour to pick them up from the runway at Obaldia? Was it connected to Rhodes? Had he sold them out for some reason that Frank had no knowledge of? The questions swirled around his brain, but he wasn't any closer to figuring it out.

Frank studied the guard, who was slumped in a relaxed position, his head leaning against a thick piece of wood that made the door frame of his hut. His head dropped slightly, and he righted himself quickly and looked over at the cage as if to check whether he was being watched. They both appeared asleep, and the guard relaxed again.

"I don't imagine these pricks are gonna play nice for long," said Nero. He shook the cage bars when the guard wasn't looking as if they might crumble at his touch but they remained firm.

Frank joined him in checking the seams and joints of the wooden cage. It seemed pretty solid, but he couldn't make any noise by kicking just yet.

Frank checked the boards they were sitting on. They appeared to be simply nailed to the main cage frame that made their enclosed prison.

"Dunno if we could roll it over, kick out the bottom," Frank muttered.

"Not with a guard watching," Nero replied, glaring at two of the soldiers chatting by one of their huts.

Frank sighed, feeling despondent. He felt angry at himself for letting this happen.

They had the cigarettes, of course, laced with Scopolamine aka "devil's breath". The soldier hadn't seen the harm in letting them keep them, bar the long-term health risks, Frank cynically mused to himself.

The lone guard sat opposite, a few metres away, sipping water. He got up and moved across the camp checking the perimeter. Frank used the opportunity to kick the bars with both feet. But there was no "give", if any movement at all.

He tried again. The bars remained firm.

Frank brought out the cigarettes, and Nero gave him a knowing glance.

"I can't smoke any of these myself – you have any normal ones?"

Nero fished around and brought out a pack he'd bought in Panama airport.

"Give me one, I'll offer him these," Frank's eyes darted to the Scopolamine laced pack.

When the guard returned, Frank had the cigarette Nero had given him in his mouth.

"*Señor*. Do you have a light? We don't have one."

The young guard paused, slowly walked over and crouched down, a plastic lighter in hand. Frank inhaled and made a show of exhaling with an expression of relief. He nodded his thanks, then held up the pack and offered the guard one, who fished one out.

"*Gracias.*"

He stood up and walked back to his spot, then sat down on his seat, placing his rifle to his side while Frank and Nero surreptitiously watched his every move.

The soldier placed the cigarette in his mouth and finally lit it, leaning back to take in his first drag.

"How long does it take?" Nero asked.

"No idea, but I think it's fast. Just hope this works."

Nero's eyes, caught by a pale moon, focused on the guard. "Sure, hope so, buddy."

Frank didn't want to screw up. If he made a move too soon, the guard might suspect. The stupefying effect – if it worked – should make him compliant to any of their suggestions.

If it worked.

They waited for five minutes, long after the soldier had stubbed out the cigarette, while they agreed on a plan in low whispers.

"*Señor?*"

The guard leaned forward at Frank's voice, then stood up and walked over, slightly unsteady on his feet. He touched his throat for a moment, then bent down, smiling at them with dilated pupils.

So far, so good.

Frank smiled back and looked apprehensive.

"Erm, I need a crap, but—" He turned his head and looked at Nero. "I'd rather go out there than in here, if you understand me?"

Nero made a face, agreeing wholeheartedly.

The guard nodded serenely.

"*Si,* I understand."

He hesitated for a moment, then unlocked the cage door and opened it wide. Frank crawled out and hauled himself up, stretching out his back and legs. It felt fantastic after all the hours hunched up inside that cage. He checked the other huts, the soldiers still inside.

"*Gracias, mi amigo.*"

The drugged guard nodded benignly and turned to Nero as he crawled up to the cage door.

With a swift move, Frank grabbed the soldier around the mouth with one hand and secured his bicep around the throat with his other arm in a classic sleeper hold. The soldier kicked wildly but his strength had been weakened by the drug, and it was easy, like throwing a dog a bone. The soldier soon slumped into unconsciousness, and Frank dragged him into the cage then relocked the door.

"Let's go," Frank whispered.

Just then a voice from one of the huts got louder as if heading to the door, a shadow from the door crack shifted and a shaft of light danced across the grass.

They ran across to the treeline and disappeared into the thick jungle. A wind rustled the trees which Frank hoped would disguise any footfall. Being quiet wading through the foliage was impossible. They moved further and further from the camp, the half moon their only source of light. It would be impossible to navigate precisely, although Frank had an idea of the general direction they needed to go. That was back to Puerto Obaldia; the nearest place resembling civilisation. It had been too dangerous to retrieve their backpacks with their legend passports and gear, but at least there was nothing in them to give the paramilitaries any leverage.

Their boots sploshed through deep ponds of dirty water as they carefully navigated their way through dense reed beds and over moss-covered boulders. The further they got from their camp, the faster they dared to move. At that moment they both heard shouting. Their escape had been discovered. Distant torchlights cut through the thick foliage, barely penetrating it as their captors began their search.

"Keep moving," Frank hissed to the dark shape of Nero, who'd stopped to look around.

"Fuck, we're screwed," he replied.

"We're not screwed yet," Frank growled. He hoped he was right.

Chapter 22

Frank wiped the sweat from his forehead. The wind had dropped. Somewhere in the distance, Frank thought he heard the sound of flowing water. With that, he realised how thirsty he was and took another swig from the bottle they had been given earlier. He handed it to Nero. That, of course, was the other vital consideration. In escaping they had found themselves with no water, supplies or weapons. They had to get back to that airstrip.

The hill loomed overhead, and they continued to brush through the undergrowth, glimpses of moonlight casting the plant life with a faint hue. Nero had slipped and nearly fallen into an abyss of darkness but was surprisingly agile and unperturbed by their new situation. Frank let him lead for a while, occasionally hissing at him to change direction. He couldn't believe how fast things had gone downhill: lost, trying to find a way back to civilisation in the pitch blackness with only the whine of mosquitoes and pursuing paramilitaries for company.

They continued, making slow progress. Frank assumed their hunters would know parts of this jungle well, certainly better than them. That, with the darkness and the rough terrain, made stopping and waiting for the dawn light tempting. As if reading his thoughts, Nero stopped and turned.

"This is insane. We should find a hide and wait."

Frank paused. It was a risk but, he had to admit, thrashing around and burning up energy in the dark was not the answer.

"Alright. If we can find a spot."

They continued up the hill and then moved along it instead. Another glimpse of moonlight from behind the clouds gave Frank a better view of a narrow indent in the hill, surrounded by bushes and trees.

"This seems good. Should hide us from visual contact at least."

They crawled through the foliage and crouched down between the clump of trees, positioning themselves so they were facing in opposite directions.

Frank checked the ground with his hand for any hidden surprises before taking a position leaning up against one of the tree trunks. From his vantage point, he could see the direction they had just come, through the dark, jagged shapes of the plants and trees. Nero had a view ahead of them, just in case the guerrilla army somehow got around that way, although Frank couldn't imagine how they would.

They sat in silence, just the sound of crickets and high-pitched sawing sound of the mosquitoes. The damp air held the combined scent of soil, vegetation and wood. For the first time, Frank consciously breathed it in with deep inhales.

"You've got powerful people very keen to talk to you, haven't you, mate?" Frank whispered.

There was a silence as if Nero was contemplating his answer. He spoke in a severe low tone.

"—to be expected, buddy. What I have is critical information. The finer details on a global agency that will operate above all governments. They've got big plans for it."

Frank nodded in the dark to himself. He wondered if it was their situation and the very real possibility of death or re-capture that was helping Nero to open up.

"Is this US-led?" Frank asked.

"It's a global thing," he replied.

"Then whoever is trying to grab us is trying to protect their investments, their little secret. Why are you taking this to Eaglecraft?" It was apparent, but Frank was testing, probing.

"There are reasons that I can't go into. But, let's just say there's money on the table, always a great incentive. Then there's the morals of the whole thing. It's a risk. I always knew it wouldn't be easy, switching over to be with David against the Goliath."

To him, it seemed the money angle was believable, but being influenced by a pivoting moral compass? Frank wasn't so sure Mr Nero had a moral compass.

High above them, the dark sky had lightened to a predawn hue giving the dark shapes of plants and hanging vines around them the more familiar contour of detail. Frank was able to finally see down the hill they had come up. All around them was a wall of thick foliage he hoped they could find a way through. To the side of them was a sharp decline where the trees followed a slope down what sounded like a ravine with the distant sound of flowing water. They fell silent, and Frank was about to suggest it was light enough to move when he caught a noise, alien to the harmonised chirps of insects that belonged to the rainforest. It had come from the direction of their earlier climb.

Like the accidental click of metal against metal.

Frank reached round to touch Nero's shoulder, signalling silence. He slowly turned his head, acknowledging Frank, and looked in the same direction. Frank levelled out his breathing and narrowed his eyes, focusing down the hill. Then there was a repeat of the same faint sound, slightly nearer.

Frank, not keen to be caught off guard, carefully and quietly repositioned himself onto his haunches. Nero followed his lead. A group of palm leaves just ten feet away slowly parted. First he saw the barrel of the rifle, then the hand holding it and the green camo sleeve. The guerrilla moved through the leaves, half crouched, slowly swiping his barrel aim in an arc. Frank recognised him as one of the younger ones from the squad. The soldier was checking the ground, and Frank wondered how much of a trail they might have left. Had he seen their tracks? Was that the reason he'd come up the hill? In which case, it'd lead the guerrillas straight to them.

Frank turned to Nero and signalled to stay put with a jerk of his finger to the ground. He moved back around Nero behind the tree in a semi-circle and crouched. The soldier, still treading carefully in kitten-walk mode through the undergrowth, moved past him and towards Nero's hidden position. The others must be near, but he had to act now. Frank silently moved from the tree, now in touching distance from his back. A sudden rush and Frank leapt, throwing his right arm over the soldier's right shoulder and locking the guerrilla's throat with his forearm. With his other hand he covered the soldier 's mouth and squeezed hard, pulling him back off balance. They both fell onto the ground. Nero didn't hesitate and came out in front of them, grabbing the AK out of the guerrilla's hands and following it with a harsh kick in his groin. A low grunt of pain came from behind Frank's left palm.

His eyes stared wide as Frank crushed his larynx, depriving the man of essential oxygen. As his strength sapped, the soldier kicked and thrashed, flailing his arms, desperate to hold onto life. Frank held on hard as the soldier thrashed and attempted to wriggle free. The struggling slowly dissipated until he fell into unconsciousness and death.

Wasting no time, Frank proceeded to search him, taking his ammo belt holding spare magazines for the rifle, a knife from a holder around his chest. There was a grenade. Inside his backpack Frank briefly saw an assortment of useful stuff including a water bottle, a roll of wire and a medical kit. There was also a wallet filled with Colombian pesos over varying denominations.

"Great, we're in business," said Frank, standing up as Nero finished off checking the AK's curved magazine before slamming it back into place.

Frank held his hand out to take it. For just a fraction of a second, Nero hesitated, then handed it over.

"That guy got anything else?" the American asked, glancing down at the dead body.

"Nope," Frank replied, setting the weapon in high port position. He checked the direction the soldier had come.

"The others must be close."

"Any idea where the hell we are?"

Frank paused, looking across the sloping hill that ran down to the ravine.

"More or less," he replied before moving off.

Descending back down the hill, they occasionally stopped at intervals to listen, then continued along the route they had come. Frank intended to continue to find a reference to get back to that village. What that might be he had no idea. They reached a point where another route leading down to the ravine and deeper into the jungle looked possible. Frank held up a fist by his head, signalling Nero to stop, and both men crouched low. He had sensed something ahead and was right to be cautious. Through an opening in the thick foliage came the sight of three more guerrilla fighters, stalking through the green shade like wraiths of Death.

Chapter 23

Frank and Nero edged back down the rocky ravine, retracing their steps as their pursuers moved onto their position. Their route was steep and rocky. Mangled trees grew out of the hill at impossible angles but at least made good supports for holding onto. Below them, a muddy slide led to a clump of rocks. Through the gaps, Frank caught a glimpse of the river they had heard the previous evening.

On one particularly steep descent, Frank lost his footing and had to grab a nearby branch to stop himself falling.

Shit!

There was a crack from the broken tree limb as he did so and both men froze. Nero glared at Frank for his mistake. Frank gestured to keep moving, and they continued down the slope.

Then, from somewhere above them, they heard a noise followed by a burst of gunfire, shredding bark and plants just behind their position.

"Down!"

Frank scrambled through the mud behind a clump of trees. He turned to see Nero hugging the floor, his hands around his head. More shouts as the shooter called his mates.

"Hey, Nero!"

The young man looked up.

Frank gestured for him to get ready and brought up his AK gun, aiming the barrel up the hill in the direction of the enemy. He caught a glance of a soldier just as he stepped out from behind a palm tree.

A burst of fire from Frank's weapon peppered the palm, and the soldier quickly fell back to cover. Frank fired another burst as Nero crawled across the slippery hill towards him. He continued moving along the natural treeline that acted as a barrier and Frank followed. They edged downwards, aiming for the rock cluster and the water.

More rounds hit their original position.

When they reached the rocks and crouched down behind them, Frank peered over and heard the shuffling feet as runners approached. He waved his free hand for Nero to continue to the river and aimed the clump of trees. A barrel appeared, an arm of a cautious soldier. Frank squeezed the trigger in a three-round burst and heard a cry as the soldier spun back out of sight.

Time to move.

Nero was stumbling between boulders, and then disappeared. Frank turned and saw two more soldiers come around the corner. He fired, hitting one in the leg, and the man crumpled.

The other saw him and began to take aim.

A crackling burst from Frank's AK stitched a bloody pattern across his chest.

Both down.

Frank turned and ran between the boulders.

The narrow brown stream rushed past and Nero was sat there, resting on his haunches, waiting for him. Frank jerked his hand to indicate downstream and continued running. They found a clear path alongside the river and followed it. Frank checked their six, keeping his eyes around and ahead. There was no reason to doubt the enemy could come from anywhere.

Was it a pincer move? Some trap?

These guys knew the jungle, and they certainly weren't stupid.

They continued for twenty minutes in a southwest direction. Frank again held up a fist and then waved a flat hand downwards for them to assume cover. They crouched, catching their breath.

"All right," said Frank through ragged gasps. "I think we're way ahead of them. Got to be careful though. They're jungle fighters. Must know this place pretty well."

Nero nodded. Frank unshouldered the backpack he had taken from the young soldier and opened it up. "I'm sure I saw a map in here," Frank said, rummaging around.

"Ah, we got a compass too." He took a look at the basic army issue device. "All right—" he added, folding out the map.

"By my estimation, we should be around here," Frank pointed at a ridge on the map, "they're probably forming a dragnet along here," his finger tapped on the curving line of a river. "There's no way to get back to that village without taking a huge detour here," Frank pointed his finger along an area inland. "By the time we do that, we may as well keep heading south further into Colombia."

"Fuck," Nero muttered, as he held his head back, rubbing his neck and looking up at the canopies.

Frank folded up the map and started putting it and the compass away. "I know, I don't like the idea either."

"What about water? What have we got?"

Frank pulled out a half-full plastic bottle and stared at it.

"No more than a litre. There should be a freshwater stream on the way, or we can hack into some bamboo trees, next time we see one. Just have to be frugal with what we've got, for now." They each took a swig and then continued moving at a steady pace, looking for a place to cross.

"This should lead to a larger river, according to the map," Frank said, tracing a path on the map. "We've got to be careful. There are still other dangers."

Nero cast his eyes around at the impossibly thick jungle.

"Dangers worse than those guys?"

"There are plenty of groups in this area; FARC use it, so do the drug cartels. The group that's after us is most likely AUC. Well, that's my guess. Plus there're the natives– keep your eyes wide, that's all I'm sayin'."

"Sounds like you know more than me. Just keep that weapon loaded."

They came to a clearing with a panoramic view of the valley and the river that looped through it like a brown snake sliding through thick grass. The terrain looked formidable, a vast untamed natural vista of endless green mounds that faded into the mist of the early morning. Frank closed his eyes for a second. This felt like his biggest challenge yet. It was precisely what he didn't want to do; head deeper into that unknown, running straight into the thick of it.

"Hey!" Nero pointed at a clump of bamboo trees just ahead. "I say we get some water from those."

Frank pulled out the knife, chose a section of the tree and began hacking a wedge into it. After a few minutes, as the clear liquid flowed out from the bark, Frank and Nero smiled and nodded at each other. A rare expression of relief. They weren't going to die of thirst – at least not yet. They gulped down the abundant water before filling their water bottle.

Just as they were about to move on, a distant noise caught their attention. It was a rapid whupping sound that faded in and out in the distance.

"Hear that?" he asked.

Nero looked up and around.

"Yeah, that's a chopper," he confirmed.

Chapter 24

The pulsating staccato of rotor blades grew louder, cutting through the dense overhead canopies. No doubt about what it was now. Certainly not anything that might be looking to rescue them. How nice would that be? Frank mused to himself.

No, they were being hunted.

"Come on! This way." Frank began fast walking along the ridge. They couldn't hide where they were for long with the guerrillas at their back, and the sound of the helicopter indicated it was getting closer, but it was difficult to locate with the surrounding rising valleys. Ahead, there was a brief stretch of open ground, then thick jungle that would make a good cover for them.

Frank glanced back to check Nero was following him and saw him stumbling. At the same moment, beyond his shoulder, a brown face in olive camos appeared in the treeline, raising his weapon. He fired and Nero grunted, spun around and pitched into the ground hitting some protruding rocks hard with a grunt.

"Hit!"

Frank jumped down onto the ground and pulled up his weapon, firing a round in the general direction of the guerrilla who immediately withdrew, calling for backup. He crawled back to Nero.

"Where?"

"Shoulder, I think."

"We can live with that," Frank said, trying to get eyes on the wound.

"I fucking can't, man. Jesus, it hurts like hell," he grunted. "Shit! Shit! Shit!" he hissed.

Frank studied the wound. "It looks like a graze, but we'll keep an eye on it."

He searched in his bag and found a basic trauma kit, pulled out a bandage and did a quick patch-up job.

"The bleeding doesn't look too bad. That'll have to do for now." Frank glanced towards their pursuers, then back the other way.

"Can you get to the treeline?"

Nero exhaled loudly. "Yeah sure. Just gimme a minute."

Distant shouts cut through the trees.

"We haven't got a minute. Keep your hand pressed on the wound and move, I'll cover."

Nero gritted his teeth as he forced himself into a crouch and ran, clutching his shoulder.

Frank took aim and looked for his target. He could see three of them spread out in different directions and fired short bursts, each time changing the direction of fire. They had dropped back into cover, and he had no idea if he'd hit anyone. Frank stayed low and followed Nero. As if from nowhere, a black helicopter appeared above the trees swooping across the valley.

"Down!" Frank shouted.

Nero was already under the trees, but Frank felt incredibly exposed as the blades whooped up ahead. The nose of the chopper tipped down exposing black-tinted windows. It turned to its side and hovered.

Running now, Frank focused on the trees. Nero had disappeared, swallowed by the thick jungle.

In the side doorway of the chopper, a woman in black swivelled a mounted machine gun around to her target.

Frank swerved his run, changing direction suddenly, his heart pounding.

This is insane. Too exposed!

Brakabrakabraka. The drill of 50mm rounds churned up the spot of his original trajectory. Chunks of debris flew through the air, raining on Frank's back.

Frank dived and rolled in the muddy ground, behind the cover of a cluster of rocks, and held his head in his hands. Swishing bullets whistled overhead, smashing fragments of rock through the air in all directions.

"Shit! Shit! Shit!" he shouted.

Brakabrakabraka. The firing continued for another ten seconds then halted.

The direction of the low whooping sound changed. They were circling to get a better shot. Frank wiped his brow and checked his magazine. From his haunches, he raised his height slowly, barrel pointing through a slit in the rocks. It hovered like an angry wasp, spitting bullets. On the ground, he caught a glimpse of the soldiers, who were trying to flank him. He fired a quick two rounds at the chopper, then bolted, skirting around them the rocks before heading to the mass of trees.

The throbbing of the chopper's engine grew nearer as it moved to get a clear line of fire on him before he hit the trees. Around ten metres stood between the rocks and the treeline. Behind him the deep cavernous drop.

Frank hurtled as fast as he could run across the gap. He heard the machine gun open up with its murderous staccato once again, just as he jumped head-first onto the jungle floor; a thick waist-high wildness.

Bark splintered and wood and shredded foliage sprayed in all directions as a wall of concentrated firepower seemed to rip the jungle apart with its deadly rain.

Frank crawled, using his elbows to pull himself along in a diagonal line, his head almost flat to the ground. His elbows, jabbing hard, felt raw.

He was dead. It was over.

Then the relentless drilling halted, and the engine changed tone as if gaining altitude.

Frank didn't stop moving. Crawling deeper and deeper to get as far away from that chopper. The ground sloped down into a ditch, and he rolled onto his side, gasping for air.

"Jesus, Jesus!" he gasped.

Frank closed his eyes and sucked in the much-needed air as a light mist rose from the ground. All his body wanted to do was stay put and rest, but he forced himself to move on. This was no time to dick around; he needed to find Nero. He rolled onto his hands and knees and looked back through the shredded jungle towards the ridgeline. Whole palm trees had been chopped in half. The machine gun had cut a wide arc like a scythe through butter. No doubt the guerrillas would be coming in to look for their bodies any minute.

Frank checked his magazine and reloaded from the bag, then looked around.

"Nero!" he hissed, trying not to shout.

A few yards behind him he heard a light groan, then he heard, "Over here!"

Frank crawled over to his position.

"Are you hit anywhere?" he asked.

"From that firepower? Don't think I'd be alive if I were. My shoulder hurts like hell, though. Need to fix it up, quick." Nero looked ghostly pale, the sheen of sweat appearing across his face. "I didn't think they wanted to kill us?" Nero added.

"Guess they do now," Frank replied. "C'mon, we'll patch it up further on but not here. The ground forces are still on us."

Frank checked behind them for any sign of the enemy and hauled Nero up to his feet by his upper arm. Ahead of them, through the constant dull green light, lay more thick trees, hanging vines ascending another hill. Frank felt the sweat almost rotting his clothes, now caked in green smears and mud.

"How long can we keep this up? Seriously. I'm dying."

"No bloody choice, mate," Frank muttered.

Nero stopped. "Hey. This is a clear route, right? There'll be no doubt we came this way. Can we do something with that grenade?"

"Like a trap? Yeah, I don't see why not?" Frank replied. He thought back to an earlier time with his mentor, Sam. A brief lesson on grenade traps. Lessons learned in the military. Simple stuff stemming back to the World Wars or the Viet Cong. Now they laid some pretty nasty traps in that jungle. They had wire and a grenade. It was worth a try to give their pursuers something to think about.

"There's wire in the bag."

"Alright. We need two stakes or something similar. Sticks will do, both sides of the path," Frank glanced around, "the grass is long enough here to hide the wire."

They found appropriate sticks and hammered them into the ground, opposite each other across the path. Frank took out the grenade, tying it to one of the sticks. Next was the tricky part. The safety pin was split with both the ends bent outwards through the fuse assembly and strike lever. Frank carefully closed down the split pin and then wiggled it almost out, so the slightest tug could remove it. Taking the wire, Frank secured one end to the pin and the other end to the far stick, stretching the wire out across the path.

When the trap was in place, they checked the wire was just below the grass line before moving off into the jungle.

Frank spat into a mesh of palm leaves as they edged through the cluster of undergrowth, both men only too aware they were leaving tracks for their pursuers.

We're against the ropes here.

Frank just hoped the ground would soon become less trackable.

They kept moving at as fast a pace as they could, navigating the clustered jungle foliage until they came to an impassable scattering of swamps, their flat surfaces mirroring the green hue of their surroundings. They moved around the edge of it and then the ground began to descend, the trees and vegetation at last becoming more sparse with rockier ground underfoot. It would be harder for the guerillas to track them now.

"Let's look at that wound now."

Nero stopped him with his hand.

"It's fine. I got it. You don't have to be my nursemaid, buddy."

Frank shrugged. "Whatever. Just tryin' to help."

"And it's appreciated, but I'd rather take it from here," Nero muttered as he pulled off the hastily applied bandage from earlier. They both looked at the patch of congealed blood where the bullet had sliced the flesh at the top of his humerus. "Like I said, a graze. Looks fine to me."

Nero acknowledged him with a nod.

Another hour and they came to a rocky trail that spiralled downwards into the same ravine they had encountered earlier, albeit farther south.

"Alright, we stick close to that river and we should be on course to get to a place called Ancandi, according to the map. Hopefully we can get supplies, maybe a ride out of here." After feeling safe enough to stop, Frank bandaged up Nero's wound with rags stripped from their own clothing. The overwhelming humidity made for the worst conditions for an injury, slowing down any healing. There was also a high risk of infection.

Afterwards, they ate the meagre rations from the backpack consisting of some plantain fruit, nuts and a bag of cooked rice. They drank more water, but the level was now dwindling in the bottle. Their situation was at crisis point. They needed freshwater fast – and not only that but they were just a few hours from darkness. There were now no bamboo trees in sight. Forcing themselves on, they hiked for over an hour, slowly descending their way down to the rocky trail.

For a brief moment, they both thought they heard the sound of the helicopter in the far distance, but it soon faded leaving the familiar jungle background track of crickets and howler monkeys. The wilderness around them seemed to be seeping into their pores, and sweat continued to soak their entire bodies. They continued stumbling across slippery rocks and past gnarled tree roots that protruded from the ground.

The sky had darkened when they reached the stream, but they barely noticed, dipping into its cool liquid haven before taking cautious mouthfuls. Frank filled their only water bottle and checked his ammo. Three rounds left. He hoped they wouldn't run into their friends again anytime soon.

He looked around their surroundings and found a spot where they could hide and rest with only one possible approach, in front of a wall of rocks. Not ideal, but it would have to do. Both of them needed at least a few hours' rest otherwise they would be falling over their feet. They took turns as the night sky descended, but the mosquitoes made rest fitful. Without any repellent, both of them were getting eaten alive. They covered themselves up as much as possible. Then Nero suggested they covered their exposed skin with mud from the river bank which kept the biting down to some bearable level.

As soon as it was light enough, Frank rechecked the map, as well as their bearing with the compass. If they were definitely in the location he thought they were, it meant a riverside village lay twenty klicks away. If all went well, they could be there before nightfall. Whether it was safe was another question.

They headed off again, transversing the stream and setting a steady pace, strengthened by the intake of water. Despite it being dawn, dark and foreboding clouds swirled overhead. The heavy *drip, drip, drip* began to patter on the plant leaves around them.

"Don't suppose you brought an umbrella?" Nero asked, barely managing a smile.

"Left it back at the hotel," Frank answered. Nero laughed then. "If we ever get out of this. Well, I might even buy you a lemonade."

Frank couldn't help snort. "Thanks, mate. That's given me the spur I need to get the hell out of here."

They walked in silence as the rain grew heavier, growing into a rumble as they came to a section of the jungle that stood in their way. Frank attempted to hack reeds and a mass of hanging vines aside with the butt of his rifle with little success.

"So, you worked for one of the British intelligence services, I understand," said Nero.

"Something Rhodes told you?" He didn't bother with codenames. They both knew who they were working for. The need for secrets and caution seemed like another world, far away.

"Don't worry. He didn't give you away. But I needed some assurance who was bringing me in and carried out due diligence. Can't be too careful, right?"

"Right." Frank concurred.

Moving off from the impasse of the jungle they came to a ridge and below, just as Frank had hoped for, they saw the village, a ramshackle mesh of stilted wooden houses and canoes tied up to the trees. Wooden steps descended into the river, a sloped small patch of mud like a dark beach hosted a row of motorboats. A few figures moved around and the unmistakable shouts from children who played on the riverbank.

Nero lightly slapped Frank's shoulder. "You saved us, buddy!"

Frank stared emotionless down at their apparent salvation. Something told him the danger was far from over.

Chapter 25

As the waves of torrential rain came down, the two men made their way towards the village. It wasn't a straightforward route and took more than an hour. The black mud stuck to their boots, forcing them to tread carefully or risk stumbling over in the quagmire. Finally, soaking wet and exhausted, they came to a more well-worn track, the first buildings of the village in sight.

"So, what's our story?" asked Nero.

"Just lost travellers. I think this place might be controlled by FARC so we have to be careful. I might have to hide the weapon."

"Sure."

It was a calculated risk, but Frank felt they had no choice. The need for supplies and help battled against the fear of danger. They found a sheltered nook under a rock and hid the AK-47, along with the camouflage backpack, before approaching. A child of around five saw them first, turned and ran back. A black man sheltering under a corrugated sheet that jutted out from one of the stilted houses waved and shouted. "Amigos!" A positive start. Frank waved back and they continued, seeking shelter from the downpour. A group of children ran up to them and followed their progress, pointing and laughing, apparently unconcerned about getting soaked in the rain.

"*¿Dónde está la tienda?*" Frank asked, looking for someplace to get help. One of the older boys tugged at Frank's arm and ran ahead, splashing through the puddles.

As they moved deeper into the town, passing clapboard houses on stilts, a few of the villagers turned and stared. Another man by the river tying a boat glanced up for a few seconds, then returned to his task. The boy scurried up to a door of one of the wooden houses, up the steps and inside, then turned and waved them in.

Frank and Nero trooped up the steps and into a dry goods store that appeared to cater for foolhardy jungle treks. An elderly woman, dark-skinned with jet-black hair, looked up at the strangers and smiled. The two men returned the greeting and stared up at tinned sardines, tuna, beans as well as packets of pasta, rice and coffee. They grabbed bottles of water, food they could consume easily like rice cakes and empanadas, along with bars of chocolate which they ate while picking out their supplies. The boy disappeared. Fish hooks and plastic tarp were also added to the pile. After stacking their new supplies and getting the price, Frank took off his belt that had become partly mouldy and unzipped a hidden section on the underside, fishing out carefully folded-up US dollars for payment.

He paid, then asked the woman if anyone could take them down the river in one of the canoes they'd spotted. She asked if they were migrants. More were flooding through, heading up to Panama to try and get to the USA.

"No, just backpackers on an adventure trail – we lost our way," he replied in Spanish, followed by a shrug as if to say, "idiot gringos".

She laughed. "The commander will come. They give permissions for travel here," she said. Frank paused, a tin of beans in his palm.

A commander. That didn't sound good.

"Who is the commander?"

"*Señor Jiménez.*" She pointed and, as if summoned out of thin air, a rough-looking man stood in the doorway, dressed in green fatigues with a rifle slung over his shoulder. He strolled into the store, surveying the strangers. He was a short, squad figure with a shaved head.

"*Buenos dias*," Frank started, trying to keep it light.

The commander nodded but said nothing, circling around to look over their supplies.

"Where are you from?" he asked in English.

"I'm English, he's American," said Frank, thumbing at Nero, whose eyes darted between them. "We were trekking but got a bit lost." He glanced at the commander's jacket badge; the emblem with FARC-EP and an outline of Colombia backed up by the colours of yellow, blue and red and two rifles crossed. The uniform similar to the guerrilla fighters that had kidnapped them, but with a different dispersive pattern.

Frank understood enough from the background files on Colombia that FARC had fought a war with the Colombia state since 1948. Not only that, but the right-wing AUC was their sworn enemy.

The commander's eyes switched to the bloody patch breaking through from under Nero's ragged shirt. He looked up at Nero, awaiting explanation without a word.

"We were attacked by soldiers," Frank interjected.

The commander eyed Frank with sudden interest. Frank described them vaguely. "They had badges, ACU, something like that," he said, casually, deliberately getting their name wrong.

"AUC? Autodefensas Unidas de Colombia?" the commander asked, staring hard at Frank, his features darkening.

Frank nodded as if thinking about it. "Right. Sounds like them."

"You come with me. You can get your things, later," he said, almost as an order before walking outside. Frank and Nero gave each other a look as they followed him out into the continuing deluge. The commander walked only a few metres before stopping at another wooden house and gesturing them up a short ladder. They climbed up onto a flat layer of planks and an ample space. Another three soldiers, two of them female, sat cross-legged, their dark eyes assessing the gringos as they climbed inside. They were striking in their appearance: beautiful and so young but, in that instant, Frank could tell from their faces that they had seen horrors to last a lifetime. A number of sleeping bags were strewn around the floor along with army backpacks as if a whole squad of them were staying there.

The commander ordered one of the female soldiers to find the medical kit. Frank and Nero sat themselves down, cross-legged at the commander's gestures. The commander poured two tin mugs full of black coffee and handed it to his two guests, as it now appeared. They took them gratefully and gulped down the hot liquid.

"*Muchos gracias*," Frank said, wiping his lips.

"So you were attacked by AUC. Where?" he asked.

"North. Nearer the Panama border."

"It's strange they are operating up there."

Frank made a face as if he had no idea why either. "It was very scary. They saw us, we ran, and they shot my friend, but we managed to escape."

The commander appraised them both, impressed. "You were very lucky, *señors*. Very lucky." He poured himself a coffee. "You do know that you are in FARC territory now. You cannot travel here without permission." He spoke as if going through the motions.

Frank dropped his head slightly, "I know and we're very sorry. We didn't know where we were."

"If you survived an attack by those *bastardos* death squads, then you are welcome here." He then gestured to them both. "And your clothes – you can dry them out here."

The young soldier returned from rummaging around in one of the bags and gestured to Nero to remove his shirt.

The commander offered around cigarettes. Frank paused, then declined. Nero took one and grinned.

"Those bastards," the commander continued, warming to his theme, "they come here two years ago. The people, they run. One man, he stayed. They chopped off his head and played football with it." He spat on the wood beneath his feet. "Animals. All of them!"

Frank nodded gravely. "Animals."

"So, where will you go?" he asked.

Frank thought for a moment. What to reveal and what not to. He decided on the truth.

"With your permission, to the mouth of the Cacaricas would be good. From there we try to get across to Apartado or somewhere on that road, or down to Domingodo. We should've just taken a plane the whole way."

The commander smiled. "We see many gringos, also migrants all flow through here. Some go into the jungle and never leave. Never seen again," he said with an air of menace. He drained his coffee, then added, "Comrade Isaza can take you there in a piragua canoe when it stops raining." He gestured to the male soldier who had watched the conversation in silence.

Frank glanced out of the door space at the torrential rain and wondered when exactly that would be.

Chapter 26

Several days earlier, Wexhall felt he had been running a very tight ship and, despite the apparent setback of the mole running around loose, it could only be a matter of time before the situation was resolved. It had to be, surmised Wexhall. They had excellent people on the ground and were steps behind their prey.

The fingerprints found in Lee's house and the ones they had on file did not match. So either he used fake biometric prosthetics when he joined G13COMM or in his daily life. Was one his real print or both fake? So far nothing had come up on either, but these things took time.

Additionally, their monitoring systems that connected the G13COMM station with the satellite surveillance might of Echelon, the signals intelligence (SIGINT) collection and global analysis network, had pulled in some impressive results. The facial recognition system had flagged another sighting of Nero, at Panama airport. That, with access to the flight manifests brought up their identity legends on a plane from Albrook airport, giving Wexhall a specific destination: Puerto Obaldia, a tiny village with an airstrip close to the Caribbean coastal border with Colombia.

It seemed perfect. Elvira was in the Caribbean, so he issued another message ordering her to proceed to Panama.

Then he had pulled out some numbers in his black book. Apart from FARC, South America was a hotbed of militias and groups funded by various US interests. Wexhall had his own contacts and pulled out the details of an acquaintance; Colonel Moreno of the paramilitary and drug trafficking group Autodefensas Unidas de Colombia.

Now, though, Wexhall was looking at a situation that had drifted into dangerous waters. The targets had escaped and it sounded like his idea to connect Elvira with the AUC was not working out. They were ripping the jungle apart looking for them, but there was a genuine possibility they had lost the trail and the cap on his operation was potentially going to be blown wide open.

He needed a backup plan and knew just the man to help.

Dean Wexhall picked up his encrypted phone and dialled the number for Carl Paterson.

Chapter 27

The following day the young soldier, Comrade Miguel Isaza, with tattoos covering most of his neck and face, expertly guided the Piragua canoe, fitted with a small outboard engine, downstream. On either side of them, the jungle closed in like monstrous green walls, with trees arching over their route visibly shaking as Howler monkeys screeched in their direction.

Miguel explained in Spanish that they should look out for crocodiles, who had been known to tip canoes over when attacking. Both Frank and Nero looked into the dark muddy water with trepidation. Warming to his nature lesson, Miguel also claimed to have seen jaguars on the banks.

Frank and Nero exchanged glances once again, happy not to have encountered any – so far. They weren't out of the jungle yet, it seemed. Although they had new supplies, the decision was made to leave the AK and the bag where it was. There was no way to explain that to the commander. It would have put a different spin on their whole conversation and probably the outcome of their situation.

****

Commander Jiménez and the remaining FARC unit also prepared to leave their base. They usually kept an eye out for any army patrols coming up the river to show the people they still had a grip on the area. Recent incursions and probes by the regular Colombian army and the

AUC had put immense pressure on the guerrilla group. The leaders had suffered a series of fatalities, losing many of their top commanders to assassinations and capture.

Commander Jiménez got the men and two women in his unit to fill up the two boats for them to move upriver to the next village. They would meet Comrade Isaza there after he had dropped off the travellers. Jiménez wondered if they were just foolish adventurers, clueless gringos. He had seen enough of their type, even kidnapped a few of them for ransoms from their wealthy families in America or Europe.

But these men looked like they could handle themselves, especially the one who called himself Frank. Something in his eyes told the commander he'd been in many tough situations and survived.

He shook off the thought as he stepped outside from one of the shacks and caught a repetitive hacking sound coming from behind the hill, which faded and then grew louder. He called to his soldiers.

"*Helicóptero!*" He gestured for them to get away from the boats.

A Colombian army attack hadn't happened in this area for years. How had they got so far north?

From the track further up, still thick with mud from the rainfall, came a shout:

"AUC! AUC!"

A jagged cracking sound bounced off the trees and the man fell, hacked down by bullets that ripped into his back. The commander turned and signalled to his soldiers, who were fanning out with AK-47s at the ready, making for the single row of houses. At that moment a black helicopter appeared, hovering just fifteen metres above the river line, the main door flung open.

Its heavy machine gun fire hacked into the ground, the arc of bullets churning up the mud on the riverbank, then mowing down the FARC soldiers like ninepins. The commander dived to the floor of the house as the wooden flats were pulverised by the chaingun hammering his position. He held his hands around his head and prepared to die. After a few minutes it fell quiet except for the low hum of the chopper that faded as if it were moving away.

He rolled onto his side and held his palm up. It was red from blood. He checked his chest, legs and arms and felt the wet patch around his thigh. He had been hit in the leg. Then the pain hit, and he found that he was unable to get up. A creak from the door and he turned to see an AUC officer sweeping his weapon barrel around the room before settling his aim.

***

The commander found himself surrounded by the soldiers of the AUC. Two of them hauled him to his feet, and he grunted with pain from his leg wound. A fist connected a massive blow to his face forcing him to reel backwards, still supported by unseen hands. Another punched his face again, causing a stinging rush of pain throughout his jaw and neck followed by a metallic tang of blood in his mouth. The punches continued to rain in, pounding his face, then stomach.

Mercifully, he lost consciousness. Then came round to shouts. He felt himself being dragged outside, his feet trawling across the ground until he felt his body thrown onto the mudbank.

It was the smell he noticed. The smell of death. He struggled to open his eyes; they were so swollen it was as if they were welded shut. Through slits, he saw bodies. So many bodies. His soldiers. Villagers. Children. A toddler crumpled, limbs at an unnatural angle, against the tree trunk he had been flung at.

He had failed, failed to protect his territory from these scumbag death squads, whose strings were pulled by the narcos and the ultra-rich in Medellín and Bogota. A drill of machine gun fire burst from another one of the stilted houses behind him.

Another murder.

He curled up in the foetal position waiting for another rain of blows. "Commander Jiménez."

The FARC commander slowly opened the slit of his eyes, surprised to hear his name. He felt a stick prod his face, forcing him to look upwards. A short man with a vicious smile looked down through mirrored sunglasses. Beside him was a woman with tied-back blonde hair, dressed in black fatigues.

A moment later an AUC soldier stepped forward and proceeded to pour liquid over his face and body. The commander coughed and jerked his head to try and avoid the stream of what he realised was gasoline, stinging his skin.

"Tell me where the gringos are."

Ah, the gringos.

The man with the mirrored glasses crouched down to better hear his answer.

"What do you say, commander? Do you intend to burn right here on the riverbed for their benefit?"

The commander forced himself to focus and could see his reflection; the battered face, purple and puffy, caked with sticky blood. He already knew his decision. They were going to burn him, whatever he told them.

So he would tell them nothing.

Chapter 28

Apparently the situation was delicate enough for the Americans to cross the Atlantic and that gave Carl a feeling of confidence. What it was they actually wanted had not been disclosed yet but he could hazard a guess. Word had obviously got around that his man – Bowen – was in the field.

The call from Stark demanding a meeting in their most secure location in London irked Carl, but he went with it and made arrangements for them to come to the Limehouse studio.

They walked in and were quickly ushered to the meeting room where Carl had spoken with Frank just weeks before.

When Carl walked in, Wexhall wore an unsettled, impatient expression and cut through the pleasantries.

"Paterson! About damned time! You think we can get some coffee around here?"

Carl was about to bark back, tell him this was his turf and to stick his demand up his backside, but merely nodded, face tight as he picked up the phone.

"Sure, colonel. But I'll warn you, it's shit coffee, and that's without me taking a crap in it," he muttered, without humour, trying to break the dynamic Wexhall was setting.

"Sure, I'll take it how it comes —" Wexhall, replied, seemingly not hearing him.

Carl grunted into the phone in low tones and slammed it down before crossing his arms.

Wexhall leaned towards Carl. "This asset of yours, he's in play right now?"

Carl raised his eyebrow at the directness of the statement, but it didn't surprise him. This man was a blunt instrument, judging by their first meeting on US soil. He resisted inhaling through his teeth like a tradesperson overestimating the price of a job and lightly brushed the table with his palm instead.

"Why do you want to know about our asset? Is this an information-sharing request?" Carl asked in as casual a tone as he could muster.

Wexhall fixed a steely glare at Carl that he briefly imagined boring a laser right through his head onto the wall behind. "Information sharing is always welcome, Carl. But it may come to something more...involved."

Carl remained impassive. "Involved?" he repeated. "Sounds expensive," he added.

Wexhall stood up suddenly, pushing away the chair as if it annoyed him and towered over Carl for a second before turning to pace the room.

"Alright. I'll level with you. The situation is this. We had a leak at G13COMM; an operative took some sensitive data, and along with everything they know about our little enterprise, they are a clear and present danger. It's a situation that needs tidying up, quickly. We have our own players in the field of course," he glanced briefly at Stark who met his eyes with a steel-like determination, "but I'm hedging my bets right now. It's a tricky situation and I need you to start pulling some levers from over here, if you get me?"

This was interesting, to say the least, thought Carl. Still, he had leverage.

"What about me? In the scheme of things?"

Wexhall gave him a knowing smile. "I didn't come here expecting something for nothing, Carl. No, the world doesn't work like that; not our world. Give me what I want, and I'll make sure you get a seat at the table."

Carl nodded, resisting a wry smile at that. It seemed all his Christmases had come at once.

Chapter 29

Frank and Nero departed from the canoe at Puente America, another riverside village that was just a strip of shacks perched on a muddy bank. Comrade Miguel Isaza helped arrange another boatman for them, before getting himself ready to head upriver. They received a hot meal of crocodile stew from one of the locals as they waited for the boatman to come back from whatever errand he was on. Frank managed to get a look at another map that one of the locals had pinned up on their wall. As far as he understood, they were still deep in FARC territory. There was also the Urabenos, a murderous drug gang that operated in the area. Frank sighed and wiped his hand through thick, greasy hair. They were still cut off from any communications. No one in this cauldron of menace and isolation seemed to have a phone or way of communicating with the outside world at all.

It was frustrating as hell. He still had to get Nero to Medellín. That had been his last communication order from Rhodes in Panama City. But now it had turned into a hellish nightmare that didn't want to end. That helicopter and the AUC group had really wanted to take them down. Although they had lost them for the moment, Frank knew they could never keep a low profile in a place like this.

***

When Comrade Miguel Isaza reached his village, he knew something was wrong from over twenty-five metres away. A waft of smoke drifted across the river and there was an eerie silence. As he drew closer, he could see the riverbank strewn with bodies. An overwhelming sense of evil stalking the nightshades enveloped him. A terrible act that would live on in memory for anyone affected by it.

Miguel cut the engine and drifted closer to the bank a few metres away, reaching for his rifle as he slowly stepped off the boat. He made his way in a half crouch, sweeping his barrel from left to right, seeing only the staring eyes of the dead, the blood in pools mixing with the muddy ground. As he rounded the corner of the first shack, there were three of the children, face down in the mud. He knew all their names. What monsters had done this? But, of course, he knew, deep down. Who else could it be?

He saw the camouflage uniforms of his comrades laying scattered around the canoes on the bank as if mown down in a line; half of them were women. These were the comrades he had lived, worked and struggled with all of his adult life. He slumped down, hardly believing his eyes.

Dead. All dead.

Then he looked up and saw the bodies of the villagers and the children.

The smoke that he thought was the remnants of fire came from a charred corpse curled into a foetal position. When he stepped closer, Miguel recognised some of the blackened uniforms. Part of the face was still visible. The ear and jawline was the only part recognisable of his commander.

"Would you like to join him?"

Miguel swung around at the voice. It came from the darkened shadow of one of the shack doorways and in the gaps between stood a line of AUC, all aiming their weapons at him. A stout man with mirrored sunglasses stepped out, one hand behind his back, holding a stick. He jutted his head. "You'd better put down your weapon, *hijo*."

Miguel did so, dropping it onto the ground, his eyes darting to the soldiers lined up against him.

A sudden fear gripped his entire body. Never before had he faced the enemy this close. Without his comrades, he felt naked. He muttered prayers, his lips barely moving.

The AUC man walked up to him, his soldiers just a few steps behind. He booted Miguel's rifle away, which was immediately picked up by one of the men.

"What is your name, soldier?"

"M–Miguel," he stammered.

The AUC man smiled warmly as if the boy was his son and placed his hand on his shoulder.

"Tell me, Miguel. You took two gringos somewhere, si?"

Miguel nodded vigorously, realising this was about them. They wanted those men. Clinging to the last strands of hope, Miguel convinced himself they might let him live.

"Gringos? Two men. Yes, jungle trekkers."

AUC man sneered, turned his head and spat onto the charred corpse of Miguel's commander.

"Where did you take them, Miguel?" he asked, patiently.

Miguel was gently sobbing now. He told him what he wanted to know, then dropped his head. The AUC man with the shades clicked his fingers, a soldier stepped up with a jerry can, and all eyes turned to Miguel as he began screaming.

Chapter 30

The boatman called Zafro had finally arrived and appeared happy to take them further south in return for dollars. They agreed on a price and hauled their new supplies aboard. Zafro ran into one of the buildings, a flatboard abandoned schoolhouse then returned and clambered in.

Frank immediately noticed he had a pistol tucked casually into his shorts belt.

"For protection?" Frank asked in Spanish.

"*Si.* Many bad men."

Frank couldn't have agreed more. It seemed like they were in very shark-infested waters. He felt edgy without a weapon but was happy to see Zafro was packing.

Zafro fired up the engine and they headed down the broad river, the main artery into the heart of the jungle. They navigated along the river for a few hours until the darkness threatened.

"We stop and eat soon," Zafro said, pointing to the banks. "I know a place."

He pulled over at a row of three abandoned shacks that was often used as a stop-off for river travellers. They brought in their bags and a jerry can of gasoline and went into one of the huts. Inside, hammocks hung on the walls, a couple of old stools and a kerosene lamp in the corner. Graffiti was sketched out on the walls, an old discarded T-shirt and plastic bags littered the floor.

It was a simple but welcome shelter for the weary.

They ate sardines from a tin, sipped bottled water then lit the gas lamp and covered the gaps in the door to keep the insects away as best they could.

"You live in Puente America, Zafro?"

"Sometimes. I travel around, always on the boat."

"Makes you a good boatman," said Frank.

He nodded and smiled, smoking a cigarette. "We go at first light."

"Sounds good," Frank said. He moved the jerry can close to his sleeping spot, and they settled down for the night.

As the others drifted off, Frank went through their supplies. From what he recalled from memory of the map, the river led down through the left side of Colombia. A place called Domingodo ran parallel with a highway route that ran into the mountainous region of central Colombia and to Medellín, more or less. The problem was the sixty or so kilometres of jungle and lack of transport options in between.

Frank yawned and rested his head on the wall boards, listening to the light breathing of the others along with the usual night noises from the forest.

***

It was just before dawn. Moreno, his two best men and the female agent sent from his employers, were heavily armed in two canoes each fitted with 5hp outboard motors. As suspected, the FARCO kid told them where the gringos had been dropped off before he had personally ended the son of a whore's life. At Cacaricas one of his many eyes and ears, a boatman called Zafro, had approached him relaying that he had just left them at a rest stop. There weren't too many other options for many hundreds of kilometres.

He was close. Very close.

It was a shame their chopper couldn't be used to continue the hunt; the fuel for it was low and they hadn't time to replenish it. He needed to continue by any means necessary, primarily as the cash bounty for the gringos was such a large sum. It would ensure he could retain his position within the AUC forces, perhaps even help him make a bid for a higher command and do much more business with the narcos that had created the paramilitary force.

As they approached the next known rest stop, Moreno ordered the engines to be cut as the canoes slid silently along the final stretch. In the distance, they could all see a single lamp hung outside the first shack. With a clenching gesture of his hand, Moreno stopped the boats on the riverbank, less than a kilometre away. They disembarked and tied up the boats.

"Gomaz, you." He pointed at Evira. "Make your way to the front of the huts, check each one in turn." He turned to the second soldier. "Restrepo, head to a position behind the huts and keep your eyes out for them."

"I'd rather take the back route," said Elvira, icily. "And why would they leave a light outside? There is something—"

"Take off and do what I tell you. You're under my command here," he hissed in reply. He had not agreed with her being part of their hunting team, but that was what his employers wanted. As far as he was concerned, a woman should be at home with kids, scrubbing the floors, although he had to admit she wasn't a bad fighter from what he had seen.

"They're just stupid gringos. Probably afraid of the dark," he added. She stared at him long and hard but said nothing.

"Alright," he said, turning to the others, "I'll be just behind you. Vamos!"

Elvira and the two men moved along the river edge for a few metres, then Restrepo split off heading into the trees to get behind while the other two pressed on and stopped just shy of the huts. Gomaz turned to Elvira, who jerked her chin for him to continue.

Half-crouched in stealth mode they silently edged along the front of the huts. Gomaz took a position outside the first hut door and nodded to Elvira who proceeded to slowly open the door with the butt of her rifle. Then Gomaz ran in, his AK-47 in firing position.

All clear.

Gomaz quickly came out as she jerked her head to the side toward the next one. The soldier then tried the handle and opened it with ease.

Crouched low, Elvira moved inside her rifle at the ready.

All clear.

She backed out as a smell of something caught her nostrils...

At the last hut door an orange glow radiated from inside. Crackling wood.

"Wait—" she began, but Gomaz hurled his shoulder against the door which gave way to his impact easily. There was a crash, and Elvira just caught a series of snapshot images as if time stopped. A glimpse of the naked flame from a kerosene lamp. A jerry can clattering to the floor, spilling its contents – the gasoline she had smelled. Then a loud "whoomph" as a rapid escalation of fire engulfed the interior as well as Gomaz.

Elvira stumbled back, covering her face from the sudden onslaught of heat, tripped and fell to the ground. She sensed a dull thud as her head hit something hard.

Her senses dulled, apart from the sound of the fire. She came around as agonising shouts gnawed at her senses. Elvira crawled away from the raging heat, coughing as her lungs burned with the acrid smoke. Her fingers gripped at the ground beneath her, head spinning. She needed to get up fast. As she lifted her head, she saw Gomaz had somehow made it to the river and had crawled halfway back out, his blackened uniform still smouldering.

Then Moreno stomped up the bank, pistol raised at the huts, his face contorted with anger. He shouted something she couldn't hear.

Over the roar of the fire, now rapidly spreading, Elvira heard a buzzing and realised it was a boat engine – no, two. Their boats! Moreno stopped and turned, looking into the darkness. A perfect target, silhouetted against the blaze of the huts behind him.

"Get down, you idiot!" Elvira shouted.

Too late.

A strafe of bullets erupted from the faint shadows of the boats. Moreno managed one useless shot at moving shapes before dropping to his knees as bullets ripped into his chest and neck. He clutched at his throat with one hand before slumping down into the mud as a stream of burning gasoline from the fires behind him snaked towards his prone body.

Elvira crawled to a clump of grass, her only available cover, the flames almost licking her feet from behind. Her AK was too far off, dropped on the ground somewhere. She pulled a handgun from her holster and aimed into the darkness. The sawing of the engines seemed further away, but she couldn't tell where they were, then she spotted the shapes on the far side of the vast river and fired off a couple of rounds. At this distance, it would only be a lucky shot to hit anything with a Glock 13. There was a flash from a muzzle and a return burst of fire sending bullets in her direction causing her to flinch and duck down to the ground. Then it stopped and the boat engines faded into nothing, swallowed up by the night.

***

A few hours earlier, Frank opened his eyes with a jolt, as if something was badly amiss. Had he just heard a boat engine in the far distance? He concentrated on the sounds but heard only the light buzzing of the jungle.

Then he noticed Zafro had disappeared and cursed himself for drifting off to sleep. Frank had suspected Zafro might be a "tip-off" guy on seeing his gun but had stupidly dismissed it. How else could someone like him afford such a weapon unless he was working for the gangs? Frank got up and shook Nero awake.

"We've got company, and our guide's gone. I don't think he went to get us breakfast."

"Great. Who's he gonna tell?"

Frank thought for a moment, his eyes dropping down to the jerry can that Zafro had forgotten to take. It had been too close to Frank, and he surmised the guy hadn't wanted to risk waking him. Outside was quiet, just the distant whining of the mosquitoes. Frank stared out into the slow-moving water through a gap in the door and heard a distant sound like splashing.

He held his hand up, motioning to Nero to keep quiet.

"I think someone's coming," he whispered. He held a finger to his ear. The sound was unmistakable; approaching boats. Although Frank knew slow-moving water always carried sound further, so he knew they had a little time. Five minutes max, in his estimation.

The chairs in the end hut; wood. And the jerry can.

Frank grabbed the jerry can and a kerosene lamp then they moved silently to the last shack of the three at the end of the row.

Once inside, Nero shut the door and Frank looked around. There were a couple of old stools and little else.

"Break one of them up for a fire distraction," said Frank, in short, clipped tones. Nero nodded and gave an OK sign. The stool broke apart easily, half-rotted from the jungle humidity. Frank grabbed the wood and built a pile in the middle of the room then poured a small amount of gasoline onto the broken wood and across the floor. He unscrewed the glass from the kerosene lamp, placed the other stool in front of the door and the jerry can on top facing inwards. It was possible just the fumes from the hydrocarbons would be enough to ignite a fire if it splashed across the floor, but the naked lamp would ensure it happened. The side window had a shutter that Nero eased open before climbing out.

Frank watched the river through the gap in the door, the silhouettes of two boats gliding closer on the muddy water. Then they disappeared behind a clump of trees, pulling into the bank a hundred or so metres away, leaving just the sound of Frank's heartbeat in his ear and the jungle crickets. His instinct was right. They were coming. He did a rough estimation. They were about two minutes away.

Frank climbed out and signalled to Nero, who had hidden amongst the thick foliage and trees. Half-crouched, they made their way into the jungle. They started to move in a semi-circle around the rear of the huts, heading in the direction of the river bank.

Frank, having taken the lead, held up his fist on hearing a noise nearby and they both crouched. Someone was approaching. The two men hid at the approaching footfall as that someone was not doing a great job of disguising their position.

There was a distant "whoomph" followed by the sound of crackling and a change of light; an orange hue lit up the trunks and vines from the direction of the river, quickly followed by a shout.

The party had started.

A soldier appeared, AK in hand, clear to see in the new light. He looked in the direction of the commotion and picked up his pace. Frank pounced from behind, grabbing his throat with one arm and jaw in the other. With a vicious twist and a crack, the soldier's body slackened and fell onto the ground. Nero helped him drag the body into the undergrowth before they stripped him of anything useful. There was the AK-47, an old Soviet Tokarev TT-33 pistol and a box of rounds along with other essential supplies in his bag.

Within a minute they were moving again, Frank checking the AK was loaded before they came across two boats tied up.

Ahead, Frank could see the glow glistening on the river surface as he untied the rope.

"We've got to go past the huts, so head to the far side, then along the bank."

They both frantically began pulling at the engine cords. Nero's fired up first, and he headed off across to the far side. Frank pulled, but it didn't fire. He tried again, and it caught. He steered his boat diagonally across towards the far side, crouching low. By now, the fire was illuminating the river, but there was nothing they could do about that. Frank let the boat tiller go and aimed his AK barrel at the river bank and the blazing huts. A figure was moving along the bank. Frank pressed the trigger, forcing the weapon down as it veered upwards on the sudden burst of loud gunfire. A single shot rang out, and Frank fired another salvo, getting a better handle on the weapon now and saw the figure slump, then fall from sight before being consumed by flames.

He put one hand to adjust direction, not taking his eyes off the huts. There was no one else in sight. Then, gunshots from a sidearm, the muzzle flashes coming low off the bank. Frank returned a burst of fire, just as the huts disappeared from view, leaving only traces of flickering light dancing across the river.

***

Elvira retrieved what ammo and supplies she could from the bodies and checked her collection: a Glock pistol, her AK, one box of ammo for each and her knife. She took one last look around and headed off along the bank after the fading boat engines. There was no chance of catching them now.

From her rucksack she fished out a satellite phone and dialled a number seared into her memory. She spoke a series of authentication identifiers until she was through to a company answering machine.

"Local Indians all sick – proceeding solo. Tangos at large. My co-ords unknown but estimate a few kilometres from Domingodo on the Atrato River." As she spoke, she spotted a shape in the reefs of the bank ahead through the clinging morning mist, then movement.

She cut the call quickly and crouched low, straining to get a better look in the low dawn light.

It wasn't likely they had stopped so soon, unless engine failure. She drew her weapon and stalked the distant shape, quietly stepping closer. It came clear it wasn't her adversaries; a local fisherman was cutting up fish for his crab traps.

She smiled to herself. Her transport beckoned.

Elvira stepped out of the undergrowth and clucked her tongue for his attention; he turned with a look of surprise and froze, only managing a toothless smile before a "thunk" from her weapon dropped him unconscious onto the ground, the sound of the fall sending birds scattering from the canopies above.

Chapter 31

Frank and Nero continued their long journey and, after another eight hours heading downriver, the boats reached Domingodo, the halfway point for anyone heading deeper into the jungle where Frank and Nero had just spent their harrowing days.

At the riverside town, a row of rusty brown corrugated iron shacks lined the muddy river.

Pigs rooted around in the alleyways, while children played on the steps to the flatboard houses that advertised Colombian beer with hand-painted signs. The population, almost all Afro-Colombian, regarded the two strangers, staring at their every move as they docked their piragua canoes. Children, some naked, jumped into the river from a jetty, laughing and shouting.

After a short rest, they traded one of the boats for supplies, procured a map and moved on, following the Atrato River in its snaking path of brown mud through the dull, dense green of the relentless jungle.

Frank studied the map carefully. There was a much smaller river that split off and cut across to Antioquia Choco, towards Mutatá and the prospect of civilisation with the Highway 62 that would get them to Medellín.

Both men thought the worst must surely be behind them now. The sparse, ramshackle hamlets now made way for river towns with more signs of modern civilisation in contrast to the savagery of the jungle.

After another full day of travelling, the relatively flat town of Mutatá with shacks and concrete block buildings came into view and they both inwardly breathed a sense of relief.

They found a sparse cafe and wolfed down their first full meal in what seemed like an age. Then Frank found a clothes stall, and they kitted out on basic attire: jeans, T-shirts and new trainers. Then they headed to the main street and boarded a packed bus destined for Medellín.

***

After taking the fisherman's boat and leaving his body in the reeds, Elvira headed down the river as fast as the basic fishing boat would go. She estimated that she could only be a few kilometres behind them. Spotting the fisherman had given her an unexpected and welcome piece of luck, like a portion of juicy steak straight off a BBQ.

Elvira could sense they were close and didn't let up until she reached Domingodo. As she cruised in, along the riverside shacks, cutting the engine, she watched the other moored boats closely. An old man in a dirty yellow vest was sitting on a makeshift pier that was nothing more than a slab of wood on metal poles.

"*Senor! ¿Has visto a mis amigos? Dos hombres,*"

He gave her what she assumed was his best ladies' smile as he pointed upriver. She treated him to her own alluring glance and then sped off in that direction. On the map, she could see the route they must take. A small offshoot in the river that led to Mutatá and the highway. There was always a chance they would try to put her off their trail by continuing, but that route looked like a long way, going deeper into the jungle and, besides, they would assume she had been left long behind without transport and couldn't possibly suspect she was so close on their tail.

At the split, Elvira headed towards Mutatá without hesitation, and after thirty minutes the dark shape of a boat appeared in her sights for a moment before disappearing around the bend.

At last. They were in sight.

She felt a rush of exhilaration and then realised the sound of her boat's engine might alert them and cut it dead. She drifted along the bank for a while before restarting it and cutting on through the murky water. As the hazy clinging heat seemed to radiate from the surrounding trees, Elvira tracked her prey, staying far enough back on the journey to Mutatá. When she arrived, she dumped the boat and moved through the tepee-style houses and single-storey homes that made up the town, with the looming familiar green hills behind.

The logical place the tangos would go had to be any transport hub. In this town, it had to be a bus terminal. She asked a local woman for directions and headed onto the main street, a wide concrete road with fruit stalls straddling the middle and the occasional store, where locals lounged around on plastic seats, watching their tiny world go by. Outside a cafe that served as a central gathering point, a small crowd of people waited in a queue to get on board. Then Elvira caught sight of them in the line. A moment later they had boarded, and the coach engine fired up. She quickly looked around, assessing the situation. It would be simple enough to find out the bus destination but, beyond that, there would be no way of knowing where they would end up. She spotted a white Jeep parked down a deserted side street and beelined towards it.

***

The monotonous six-hour journey brought them through the rolling mountainous countryside of Route 62 until the bus weaved around the snaking road that descended into the vast valley of Medellín. Skyscrapers and red-brick apartment blocks clustered the lower echelons of the city and higher up across the surrounding hillside, a cluster of distant squares – the shanty towns of the city's more impoverished barrios. Visions of the city flashed by through the grimy windows of the bus. A couple of olive-skinned, shirtless men covered in tattoos hung around outside a garage where a motorbike stood, half disassembled. A woman gesticulated while talking animatedly on a mobile phone.

At Terminales Medellín, the northern bus station, both men looked at each other and sensed each other's palatable relief, as if they were perhaps at the end of a nightmare.

"Maybe I'll buy you a beer," said Nero, with a mocking nonchalance.

Frank decided to call Rhodes first, then Carl. The initial plan was to head to an address that would be given by Rhodes on arrival.

But whom to trust?

His game of playing both sides was fraying the edges of his mind.

He bought a cheap mobile phone with a disposable SIM card from a store in the terminal and dialled the number.

A female answerphone voice asked him to leave a message. "We've arrived in MDE. Had major problems with the deliveries. I need that friend's address you promised, ASAP." Frank left his number then hung up before dialling the drop number for Carl Paterson at Ghost 13 where he heard a similar message service. As he was leaving the message, there was a click and Carl came on the line.

"Where the hell are— What is your location code?"

Frank reeled off a series of numbers and letters, the cypher code for Medellín; one he had memorised.

There was a pause as Carl confirmed it at his end.

"Alright. Now, listen carefully. Take Nero to a safe house in the city; I'll give you the location. We'll take it from there."

"What's going to happen to him?"

"None of your concern, Mr Milligan, but rest assured we'll take good care of him."

Frank felt a twist in his stomach. The thought of handing Nero over to his certain death seemed particularly nauseating after everything they had gone through. The struggle they had overcome; for this?

"You're not going to let me down, are you?" Carl asked, his voice full of suspicion.

There was a pause before Frank answered.

"Would I ever?"

Carl snorted. "Because there is an alternative: you solve the problem yourself. You have the means at your disposal, I'm sure," Carl said, his tone level and deadly.

"What about Liberatus? Won't this screw up that whole plan?"

"This is more important now. Things have changed."

Frank swore under his breath and looked across the bus terminal at Nero sitting on a bench, smoking. He met Frank's stare, smiled and nodded.

He would be stabbing the kid in the back.

He turned away, strolling in a circle.

"Send me the location," he said, dryly.

Frank cut the call and stared down at his mobile screen for a moment.

Next, he tried to phone Maria but there was no answer, so he left a quick message so she'd know that he was alright. For a moment Frank wondered if she even cared, but brushed it aside. Jungle fever was catching up with him, perhaps. Frank cut the call and returned to where Nero was waiting in the terminal.

Almost as soon as Frank had killed the call with Carl, the phone buzzed. It was Rhodes himself.

"Glad to hear you and our friend arrived safely, Mr Milligan. I'll give you an address. It's good for twenty-four hours. Then we'll meet for lunch or something. I know a great cafe our friend would love."

"That would be great."

After the call, they grabbed a taxi for Laureles, in the north-east of the city; a perfect place to keep their heads down while waiting for Rhodes, it seemed. Palms lined the quiet streets, a subdued calm at odds with the busy scenes they witnessed coming in. A fruit-seller pushed a cart shouting for buyers for his *plátanos, papayas y frutas de la pasión* with rhythmic *persuasión*.

At the address, a two-storey block, an elderly Colombian man greeted them outside the front door that had a barred gate and showed them inside an apartment. He left them the keys, explained the alarm system in Spanish and then left them to it. It was basic but clean and discreet with a small terrace looking out onto the quiet street below.

On a table was a package with about five hundred US dollars and a mobile phone.

Nero slumped down on the couch with a sigh of absolute relief.

"Hope this place is safe cos I need a shitload of sleep."

Frank smiled, concurring with a nod. "I'm gonna shower, then find out what the plan is. Then we'll get some food – and collect on those beers you promised."

After he had dried off and dressed in fresh clothes left on the bed, Frank found Nero crashed out fast asleep, breathing heavily.

Frank decided to leave him to it and ventured down the street to where he found a store. He loaded up on short-term supplies, snacks and added a pack of Club Colombia beer, then headed back to the apartment. He found Nero in the same position as he had left him and slumped onto a chair on the balcony, with one well-deserved *cerveza* and stared idly onto the street.

Grey clouds swirled overhead, and a sudden flash lit up the darkening hillside for a fraction of a second. Moments later, a heavy crack of thunder rent the air. A car alarm, set off by the concussion, began beeping loudly, birds squawked wildly in the trees and in the distance a dog barked furiously. Another series of rumbles rolled across the city overhead as if anger had manifested itself through nature. Then the slow pitter-patter of heavy raindrops before a rainstorm cascaded down in sheets.

"Hey, Frank." It was Nero, dark hair dishevelled. He took the spare chair, sat down and stared out at the rain with Frank.

"Takes you back to the jungle days, huh?" he added, watching as a man rushed across the street with an umbrella that flew outwards, turning into a useless flapping device.

"Happy never to return to that place, mate," Frank muttered, handing Nero a beer.

Nero shuffled in his seat and turned to look at Frank.

"So, any word on contact with Eaglecraft? I'd like to know what my position is and be safe, although I'm not sure here is the place."

"I'm sure Rhodes has considered every angle when it comes to security."

"Evidently not when it came to travelling here."

Frank took a long pull from the brown bottle. "Yeah, well. It could've been smoother, that's for sure."

They both laughed at that.

"I hope Rhodes is paying you enough, huh?"

"Not for that hike. I hope you're worth it, Mark."

Nero nodded, as if to himself, his face turning serious. "Oh, I'm worth it, alright."

They both watched as a woman on a scooter sloshed through the cascading water on the road, followed by a white Jeep that turned off into a side street.

***

The rain had eased, but water continued pouring off the roof across the windowless holes where the guttering had not been fitted. Elvira shuffled in her position inside the semi-finished apartment block. It gave her shelter from the elements at least and from her hidden position a narrow view of the balcony of their apartment.

Her options, as she saw them, were limited.

Take them out on the street, attempt clean kills. There were two of them, and they were both well trained so that ploy could be messy.

Or wait it out. Follow them and see if any other players appeared in the game.

Elvira swigged on her bottle of water and ate a cold empanada as she considered her options, then checked through her bag. A few rounds for her Glock 13 pistol, the AK long ago dumped for having been deemed way too conspicuous to be carrying around.

Only a few rounds. She'd have to make them count and settled down for a long wait.

As the cold light of dawn struggled to break through the thick cloud cover, Elvira decided to wait and see what crawled out of the woodwork.

Chapter 32

Frank and Nero left their apartment as a blue sky opened up overhead as if the previous night's rain had never happened. They hailed one of the city yellow cabs from Carrera 70, directing the surly driver to Envigado at the opposite end of the city. It seemed much longer than the actual thirty or so minutes to Frank with the radio blaring incessantly, spewing a mind-numbing mix of inane chatter, crappy music and canned laughter. He tried to tune it out, keeping his eye on the rear mirror from his passenger seat for any tails.

They headed along the Autopista Regional that split the city in two and veered off into the enclave of Envigado, the enclave that Frank remembered from his research had been the birthplace of Pablo Escobar, the notorious drug narco, who had been killed by the Search Bloc seven years before. They exited the cab on a quiet side street a few blocks from their RV with Rhodes.

"How do you want to play this?" asked Nero, looking down the street each way as the cab screeched off.

"Carefully. We don't know whether that bitch was alone or has an army of local gun-toting maniacs with her." They started to walk up to the main road.

"We left her in the jungle, I wouldn't worry," Nero said dismissively before slapping Frank playfully on the arm, "let's eat before we meet Mr Eaglecraft himself."

Frank half shrugged, "You're probably right. Still, I want to take a recce around the park and I'll meet you in the cafe in about ten minutes. Order me breakfast?"

They split up, each taking a separate side of the road. At Parque Envigado Nero took a right turn while Frank headed straight. Two multi-lane highways ran parallel on either side of the park, lined with a mix of stores, a bank and offices. Two paved pedestrian walkways connected the two roads, and through the park trees where fruit sellers and coffee carts were peddling their wares, Frank could see a white Greco-Roman Catholic church on the far side.

***

Nero ordered two breakfasts at the counter, then glanced around the cafe. It was empty; business must be slow. Through the trees and passers-by, he caught sight of Frank heading back towards him to the cafe after his recce. The thought had crossed his mind as to whether Frank was right to be extra paranoid. Whatever, he was just following tradecraft procedure; in which case he'd better do the same and check the back entrance.

"Where's the bathroom?" Nero asked the young gringo behind the counter, who was absorbed in a newspaper.

He thumbed to the rear of the building.

"Right at the back, outside," he replied, barely looking up at his customer. Nero walked down the corridor, passing a closed kitchen door on his right, the radio blaring inside. As he came through the back doorway, he caught sight of a woman a few steps away, making to move into a position behind crates that were stacked up in the backyard.

They looked straight at each other, the recognition instant as time froze.

Nero moved at her, feigning a left punch but shifting his balance quickly and lunging with his right. She sidestepped him and jumped, spinning in mid-air and landing a high kick right in his gut.

Nero crashed into a wall and, in a flash, she was coming at him, knife drawn.

Raising his arm, Glock in hand, Frank pulled the trigger. A loud crack echoed around the enclosed yard. Elvira's body pivoted as if attempting a ballet twirl but still managed to stay on her feet.

He had shot her arm.

With one wide arced throw she threw the knife in Frank's direction with a swish. He leapt aside behind the stack of crates as the blade hit a window frame just behind him, burying itself deep in the wood with a dull thwack.

Frank crouched low and went to fire again but just caught a glimpse of her leaping over the low wall to the street. He scurried over to Nero who nodded with a pained expression, clutching his stomach.

"I'm fine," he grunted, waving him off.

Frank moved to the back entrance and checked the road, just in time to see her turning, pistol in hand, about to fire back. Frank aimed at her centre body mass and squeezed off a round sending the sound of loud cracks bouncing off the neighbouring buildings.

Her weapon fell from her hand as she slumped onto her knees, a hand clutching over her stomach. Then she keeled over and collapsed on the ground next to her gun.

Frank exhaled and stared for a moment at the motionless form. He half jogged over to her body and bent down. Her eyes, half closed, gazed skywards. With a check of her neck for her pulse, he confirmed she was dead.

Whoever she had worked for had lost a good asset, that was for sure.

Then a screech and a white Audi turned the corner, heading in Frank's direction. The sound of a siren drifted over from the main road.

Frank ran back to the cafe backyard and waved at Nero, who had just hauled himself to his feet.

"I got her, but someone else is coming. We've got to move!"

Nero looked back into the cafe. "They might have the front covered."

Both of them looked at the high concrete blocks forming high walls on either side. There was no easy way out from the courtyard to any neighbouring buildings.

"Bollocks," Frank muttered, then he trained his aim at the rear wall. "Alright, get to the front, keep an eye on my six, and I'll cover."

On the street a screech of tyres as the vehicle stopped out of sight, then the sound of opening doors.

"Frank!" It was a shout from behind the wall, followed by the word, "Fire!"

Frank's body relaxed. It was the agreed counter-sign with Rhodes.

"Fury!" he responded quickly.

Then Rhodes appeared, flanked by a Colombian man; the Audi driver he had spotted earlier.

"We've got to move right now!" Rhodes demanded, gesturing to them both with his hand.

With the approaching police siren only a block away, Frank was happy to oblige.

***

It was a two-hour drive back up into the hills surrounding Medellín on the same route they had done on the bus. They turned up a steep lane and kept going for around ten kilometres, glimpses of the sprawling metropolis behind them.

"She tracked us all the way from the jungle," said Frank. "Must have followed us in the bus and waited it out. Had a tag on us somehow." He was thinking it through, trying to figure it out, then he turned to Nero. "You handled that well. I was surprised—"

Nero brushed it off. "Just keeping myself out of harm's way. This place we're going – it's secure, right?" asked Nero, looking at Rhodes.

Rhodes turned to face him from the front seat. "We have a network of safe houses, and I have contacts in the government here and in

Venezuela. We can go through your future role after the information debrief. See how the information you provide can help us with what we're trying to do. The people who are unknowingly repressed need a counter against the rise of the state. You're playing a pivotal role in that, Mr Nero, a hero of the world's people."

Nero visibly relaxed, although his face remained impassive.

"I'm not doing it for the people," he countered.

Rhodes sighed. "Well, maybe you should be."

"I have my reasons, and it's not just about the money."

"Alright," Rhodes said in a tone suggesting he'd made his point.

The vehicle continued until they came to a fork in the road, where the lower track curved around a hillside out of sight. The car followed it around for two kilometres until they came to a terracotta-roofed finca surrounded by palm trees and a high wooden fence.

At the gates Rhodes slipped out a small grey remote. The gates swung silently open as they drove through and into a large enclosed courtyard. A grass lawn formed a semi-circle in front of the house that sported semi archways along the side, for an exterior balcony.

"Not a bad place, John," said Frank. He thought it looked like a high-class house for the aspiring rich.

"I'm not staying," said Frank.

"Please stay, Frank. It's too late to return to Medellín now."

Frank sighed. Rhodes was right, but he was eager to get home, to get back to normality and see his kids. One more day wouldn't hurt.

"OK, I'll check flights for tomorrow."

"And tonight we celebrate our coup," said Rhodes, smiling.

Chapter 33

The cut in Nero's hand, on the loose skin between the thumb and index finger, drew a pool of blood that he dabbed away with a tissue. Frank parted behind the skin with the sterilised tweezers and attempted to grip onto the microchip with the tiny pincers without success.

"Jesus, go easy, you got it yet?" Nero was taking in sharp breaths as Frank rooted around under the skin. Frank shot him a glance without moving his head, "I didn't exactly volunteer for this—"

Rhodes, standing back from the table, chimed in. "Sorry, Frank, I would have tried, but the old peepers aren't the same as they used to be."

"I'll get this, don't worry," Frank grunted. With another bite, he managed to get the object in the grasp of the tweezers and began easing it out of the blood, millimetre by millimetre, until it was free.

"Don't drop that now," said Rhodes, edging behind Frank to get a closer look. Frank was holding it up to the light, peering at the chip that looked like a miniature translucent pill no larger than a grain of rice. He then placed it down into a metal box.

"So all the data is stored on this? Impressive," said Frank. Impressive indeed, but not unsurprising.

Nero wiped the cut on his hand with an antiseptic-soaked wipe and nodded, glancing down at the chip. "Yeah, smart, right? It was a G13COMM project, the know-how gathered from some British scientist who implanted one a few years ago. They want to use them for all kinds of shit: location tracking and ID access but the technology isn't quite there yet. In their simplest form, they can hold a lot of information, and for this mission it was perfect."

"And getting the information off it?"

Nero bandaged up his hand and flexed his thumb, his face remaining hard.

"This doesn't carry the data itself. There's too much of a chance it would corrupt. There's a tiny antenna that transmits an ID key from the chip to unlock the data which is on a secure server." He allowed himself a wry smile, then looked at Rhodes, "You should have the right stuff...right?"

The old man nodded. "As you asked."

All three men moved silently out of the room into a hallway where Rhodes ushered them into an adjoining study. A bank of three screens faced them, placed on a long desk along with a plastic box filled with tech equipment sat on one of the chairs.

Rhodes moved it onto the long table and proceeded to log into a laptop, then handed it over to Nero.

"I'll do a preliminary check on the server, make sure everything is secure, connect to it, then we can unlock the key with the RFID," said Nero, casting his eyes over the screen.

"Am I needed for this?" Frank asked.

Rhodes shook his head. "This is going to take a while. Then I have to sift through all the data. I'd like you to hang around for a bit though."

Frank sighed. "Hmm, dunno. I'm itching to get home. I'll check the flights, then give Maria a call. See how it pans out."

Nero glanced at them both before returning his attention to the laptop.

***

As expected, it took several days for Rhodes to organise all the data

Nero had unlocked and have it transferred to his server. To dig deep to see what he actually had would take a lot longer. He needed Nero around for explaining aspects of what they had, to answer questions. To wade through the information: the planned operations, codes, details of the covert military teams that were in the making.

And, of course, the danger. Rhodes peered out of the window onto the hills, the shades of green lush and vibrant. Would soldiers appear from those trees? Was it a matter of when not if?

Not that he was a stranger to it all. Rhodes smiled.

Stranger danger.

No, he could handle it although there was no doubt this was several leagues above his pay grade. There was real power having these files: he now had intimate working knowledge of the agency.

As for Nero, he would need to keep a low profile. He would be a wanted man for a long time, but Rhodes would have no problem finding him a new role. Rhodes needed all the help he could get to achieve his long-term goal: building an opposition to the octopus-like global state serving its own interests with the good of humanity at the bottom of its priorities.

Dangerous work, indeed.

Chapter 34

Nero watched the main house through the window of his guest house and the cascading rain outside. There was a glimpse of a shadow from Rhodes or possibly one of the García brothers from behind the blinds. Couldn't be sure but it didn't matter.

Bowen was about to leave, and pretty soon it would be showtime. Nero had given Rhodes enough detail about the G13COMM operation. Sketches rather than the final painting, but it would be enough to discredit them and pull the plug on the whole tub of shit without putting too many American lives at risk. A fine tightrope, for sure, and one that had to be navigated carefully.

As for Bowen, Nero had felt a kinship with the man who had done an excellent job despite all the shit that had been thrown at them. They had survived out there in the jungle, and he would miss the guy.

What a close run, though. When they had been captured and caged by the AUC paramilitaries, he had recognised Commander Moreno from the previous operation eighteen months before, waiting in the AUC camp as the two leaders arrived by 4x4. Had Moreno come closer to their "cage" and recognised him, the game would have been up right then.

Thankfully, they had managed to escape that night.

Moreno.

Just for a moment, the pattering rain against the window took him right back to that day. The Ecuador mission that followed, the FARC camp raid and subsequent capture of those young fighters left to fend for themselves.

Then, the burnings.

Poor bastards.

Draining the sea to kill the fish.

Every one of those captured had been burned alive by Moreno's sadistic hand while Nero watched, more intrigued than horrified. None of them told him where their commander might have gone. Or they just blurted out random names to try to save themselves. Whether they spoke the truth or not, the covert mission had to be wrapped up fast. There was no way they could have continued the hunt for the FARC commander, Jiménez on Ecuadorian soil that day.

How ironic he and Frank had run into Jiménez in that village. The very man, he had tried to capture on that mission.

Nero had been part of a CIA special forward group to assist with ground operations ahead of the plan while the influx of weapons and military training continued unabated in the background.

While "Plan Colombia" openly assisted the de facto Colombian state with nine billion dollars in military funding, all approved by Congress, an altogether more secret plan was about to be implemented using the combined expertise of the NSA and the CIA; surveillance and elimination. In its purest form locating and hunting down FARC leaders for assassination using the latest technology from the US.

Nero moved away from the window. That was all in the rear-view mirror now, as if obscured by the rainfall itself.

Only his current mission mattered.

Nero had been summoned by the CIA Deputy Executive Director, Kate Foster, at Langley five months before. He was already trained in the deep infiltration of networks and intelligence gathering. He was a young "rough diamond" in the world of CIA field ops. Foster had called him into one of the deep windowless rooms that had surveillance and cameras spotted all around the walls.

"Do you know why you're here?" she had asked with a stony face.

Nero had slumped back on his chair with a cool gaze towards the black mirror that took up the entire wall at the back.

"Tell me, please," he said, turning his head slightly, his dark eyes fixed on her.

"We have enemies abroad in the Middle East and domestic enemies right here at home." She slapped down a paper file and opened it with a little finger. "You'll have to read it in here and remember it."

Nero leaned forward to look at it with all the enthusiasm of a mouse accidentally walking in on a cat soiree and opened up the file.

"The next page," Foster ordered, then leaned over the table and flipped the page for him. Nero looked down at a US Army colonel. A grunt. Well, that was unfair. A grunt with power and a lot of it. The colonel was staring hard at the camera, with a craggy face and shaved white hair.

"Colonel Dean Wexhall is the most dangerous man to this agency today. Do you know why?"

Nero looked at it with renewed interest, his eyes scanning the text; taking in the various occupations, history and all the rest.

"I'm shaking with anticipation," he said, dryly.

"Wexhall has established Ghost 13 or G13COMM: a new, combined intelligence and military agency that is to amalgamate the G13UK operation. A big project and ambitious enough to rival our own."

Nero whistled. "I had heard of it. This must have come from the top?"

"Pretty much. But it's all coming from a blacker than black budget. Obviously you know whose feathers this is going to ruffle?"

Nero thought for a moment, looking down at the photo of Wexhall with a deadly serious expression, then looked up at Foster. "The Boy

Scouts?" he quipped.

Foster shot him an icy look and tapped the files with her index finger. "Us! The entire fucking CIA. So familiarise yourself with this because you're going into G13COMM as our ears and you will be playing a game. Understood?"

Nero nodded, the smirk long gone.

"Your history will show a clean sheet at one of our partner security companies. When you're in, see what you can find out. We'll keep comms open during that period."

"Who am I gonna be?"

"Don't worry. We will make sure your legend is solid as stone. When you've cleared a few security levels get that data and make sure it's something we can sell."

"Sell? Are we working for the Chinese or the Russians now?"

"Not quite. The target is Rhodes of Liberatus."

"Who?"

Foster leaned over again, catching his eye with the look of a patient mother comforting a confused child. She flipped the page again, revealing a white-haired man in his late fifties or so. It was a photo taken covertly at a traffic junction, as he was about to step into a car.

"He's built an influential alternative media network that is revealing too many close truths across the board. His younger days were spent with MI6, and now he's fishing around his old contacts and trying to set up some intelligence network."

"Paid for by who?"

"We don't know, but that would be one of your tasks when you go in. Find out, but that's not your primary mission. You need to leave a nice trail that will discredit G13COMM. It needs to be blown open using Liberatus as the conduit. Nothing comes back to us. Understood?"

Nero nodded, exhaling slowly, taking it all a lot more seriously.

"When Rhodes contacts you, he'll be wary. You'll have to be convincing, show him some lead gems, a little sample of what you're offering. We'll get you some genuine covert photos to show him. If I was him, I'd have someone else run you around for a while, have you hung out to see if there are any other interested fishes."

"Great, so there's potential for a real-life shooting gallery," muttered Nero.

"When, and only when, you've delivered the payload to Rhodes comes the final act." She paused. "Then you need to take him out."

Chapter 35

Since Frank had left on Saturday morning, Nero had been waiting for the opportunity to hack into Rhodes' computer network to access any files relating to his organisation.

Now, at last, the chance had come. Rhodes had gone on one of his frequent hikes, along with the García brothers. The old man liked to stretch his legs regularly, and Nero had accompanied him once or twice at his invitation.

Nero let himself into the computer ops room with the key he'd seen Rhodes hide inside a book in the kitchen and softly closed the door. He was hoping to find more names of people involved, other locations the group occupied and, specifically, who funded them. That was a secret that had remained behind closed doors for some time.

Nero scanned the room, his attention focusing on one of the computer towers, lights flashing in the gloom.

Need to be quick.

He sat down into one of the chairs, tapping rapid commands onto the keyboard while he listened out for their return.

A noise outside spiked his attention and he jumped up to check through the blinds. He looked to the gate. Nothing. Then noticed an empty beer bottle had rolled off the outside terrace onto the ground.

He quickly returned to his work.

Just killing Rhodes without any access to this information would make it hard work for themselves when following up on any future mission to take down Liberatus. As expected, the files were mostly encrypted. It would be a headache for the geeks back at Langley to nail but that was not his problem right now.

Rhodes had the external network locked down, so Nero had to transfer any interesting files to an external USB flash drive. It was a risk, but he couldn't transmit the data without alerting Rhodes' network. He deleted the log files to hide his trail, then slipped the drive into his pocket and left the room.

Killing Rhodes was simple, Nero surmised as he returned to his guest house. They frequently conversed as the days had passed; he was gaining the old man's trust more and more. But Nero needed to time it perfectly. The García brothers were always around, and neither were at the top of their game as far as he could tell. The other consideration was that it had to appear as an accident. Still, there were numerous possibilities that Nero could think of.

Firstly, the natural option was an automobile accident. Getting access to the cars shouldn't be too difficult.

A second possibility was to get him during the morning walks and hikes. But Rhodes was a cautious man, and his guards were always with him. He knew what he was doing would attract an array of enemies.

Later that morning, Nero strolled onto the terrace, sipping ice tea. From what he could gather, Rhodes had employed the brothers through trusted contacts or he knew their family in some way. It had crossed his mind more than once as to how loyal they might be. Would they fight to the death for their gringo employer? It was an interesting question: one Nero couldn't answer just yet.

Nero took a seat at the small table and watched a pair of grazing horses in a field across the valley.

Poison? Or that zombie drug that Elvira had tried on him back in Las Palmas? Unfortunately Frank had gotten rid of it but if he could get hold of some more? Then he could slip Rhodes some and persuade him to jilt his guards. The old man would be putty in his hands.

Nero sighed. He would mull it over; let it percolate like the excellent Colombian coffee he had been enjoying. No need to rush into a decision, unless it was needed, of course. His training gave him the full confidence that he would succeed. It had been a rough ride getting here. The jungle run came to mind. Yet many bridges of trust had been established with Rhodes and his man, Bowen. Despite the G13COMM-backed muscle that had born down on them, they had survived. All the more reason to take down their little enterprise. Now he felt he was part of some internal clean-up operation. Cutting down internal enemies of the 'State', or people deemed enemies. Working deep against allied agencies. Still not his concern. He would do the job and move on.

He thought about Frank Bowen. The man was a capable opponent. Rough but resourceful and wouldn't be a pushover. He would have had to take care of him too, had he stayed around.

Fortunately, he hadn't, and Nero was glad.

Must be getting soft-hearted, he mused.

Just then Nero caught sight of Rhodes fetching something from his car and thoughts returned once again to the manner of achieving the man's death.

Chapter 36

Frank glanced at Rhodes and Nero through the side-view mirror, standing side by side watching him leave, and a huge rush of relief washed over him. Rhodes had his man and the data and would no doubt use it to throw a few spanners in the machine of the establishment.

Now he just needed to figure out how to deal with Carl. What were the consequences for disobeying him and the British operation of Ghost 13? Should he make up a story, spin a yarn about Nero being snatched from him by Rhodes? If only Carl were that naive to buy it.

Frank focused on the distant hills as the taxi weaved around the narrow streets that headed back into Medellín. There had been no flights available for several days so Frank had decided to stay in the city and look around. But he was also looking forward to getting home. To finally try to deal with all his personal shit and actually be there for his kids when they needed him.

Frank returned to the Laureles area they had previously stayed in and checked into a small hotel. Despite the heightened alertness at the time, he remembered it for its friendly local vibe. The streets were lined with trees and no one bothered him; it seemed to be a place where nothing much happened. Precisely what Frank felt he needed. The early afternoon sunshine, a steady twenty-five degrees in the city of "eternal spring", as it was known, changed into a predictable pattern of thunder and rain in the evening.

After a long delay, the line rang. A tone that sounded distant.

"Hello?"

Frank recognised the voice of his oldest son, Joe.

"Joe? It's your dad."

There was a pause and Frank wasn't sure if it was the line or Joe.

"Dad? Where are you?"

"I'll tell you all about it when I'm back...soon. So have a think about what you'd like to do. Anything you like...football matches, Alton Towers, Disneyland...whatever."

"OK, cool," Joe replied, excitement creeping into his voice.

"I'll see you really soon, Joe. Is your mum there?"

"Yeah, I'll get her."

Another pause, then Maria came on.

"Frank? Thank god. Are you OK?"

"Hi. Yeah, everything's fine. I'll be back soon. Just wanted to let you know."

Frank thought he heard a long sigh of relief.

"So you're coming home?" she asked.

"Yes. We'll work everything out. Don't worry about the money—"

A series of beeps and the line cut.

"Shit!" Frank cursed out loud.

Still, at least he'd spoken to her and Joe.

That night, around ten, Frank took to his bed and slept deeply; a series of images of him missing his flight and unable to get home seared into his dreams.

Chapter 37

Later in the afternoon on Saturday, Nero had driven towards Medellín, a few kilometres, stopping to make a phone call on the way . He then pulled into a supply store to pick up everything he needed. He pushed a trolley around the supermarket-sized store and threw in a spanner kit, pliers and a tubing cutter, then waited in his car.

After an hour of waiting, growing bored, Nero closely watched a Mazda pull up alongside and park. A man with a dark complexion, bearded with cropped hair, wound down his passenger window.

"You got a light, buddy?" he asked.

Nero nodded and got out of his driver seat, slipping into the passenger seat of the Mazda, handing over a lighter.

"Thanks. Zeus comes bearing gifts," he said, sparking his cigarette into life from Nero's lighter.

"Gifts are always gratefully received."

The beard jerked his head slightly and Nero turned to see a black gym bag on the back seat. Nero opened the rear door and took the bag, then returned to his vehicle without another word and drove back to the finca.

***

Frank awoke early and decided to call Carl from a public phone just outside a row of cafes and bars. It was time to face the music.

He grabbed a take-out coffee, then dialled the number for Carl's messaging service and waited, reciting his code number when it answered. There was a series of beeps, the cross Atlantic transfer routine, and Frank looked out onto the street.

A young couple climbed onto a scooter and took off down the road. A blare of Latin pop blasted from a passing taxi. An old torn poster for a Colombian film called *Los asesino* – The Assassin – covered an old brick building that was a half-built unfinished shell.

Carl came directly on the secure line.

"We've been trying to locate you for some time. What is your status?"

"Heading home."

"But we never received the asset."

"The asset is with your love rival, I'm afraid."

There was a pause. Whether it was simmering anger or frustration, Frank couldn't tell.

"You were intercepted?"

"No, I dropped him off."

"For fuck's sake. Milligan!" At least in his outburst Carl retained his legend cover. Another pause, and then a sigh.

"We'll deal with the consequences later. When did you last see Rhodes alive?"

Frank sipped his bitter coffee, frowning with confusion.

"Rhodes, alive? What are you talking about?"

"The asset is a sleeper agent. He's been allowing you to take him to Rhodes for a reason. To drop a certain amount of dangerous information but also to take him out, permanently."

The space around Frank seemed to close in, and he felt his heartbeat quicken.

"What?"

Was this a ruse by Carl? Frank quickly went through the options of what he could gain from this? He wanted Nero, of course, but why label him an assassin?

El asesino.

"I've had word. It's reliable, that's all I can say. He's in immediate danger," Carl said, gravely.

"If you're so sure, why are you telling me?"

"I may not be an angel, but this isn't going to help anyone."

"This isn't one of your games?" Frank asked, his tone increasing with worry.

"I promise you it isn't."

Frank was struggling to believe it. Nero an assassin targeting John, after the hell they'd endured together and the feeling of close camaraderie to have survived it.

Hard to believe, but not impossible.

The understated impression Frank had of Nero was of someone well capable of taking care of himself, not just a geek. A trained individual. He remembered the way he'd seemed calm on the *Anita* when he was grabbed from his room. The way he had handled Elvira out the back of the cafe.

Not the kid he thought he was.

"I'm going back, then," Frank said. The decision made. "This sounds like the real deal."

Carl sighed.

"Yes, and do what you were supposed to do in the first place. You get up there. Bring in the asset to us or get rid of him. It's on you."

***

Nero waited until early the next morning before making his move. Based on his knowledge of the routines at the finca, he knew the guards would disappear around two or three in the morning. He silently let himself inside the main building and found Rhode's key fob hanging up in the kitchen, then headed over to the stand-alone garage and went inside.

Carefully closing the door behind himself, Nero glanced around inside. The Audi took up most of the space and, against the back wall, a tarpaulin half covered a motorbike, the bottom of the wheel just visible. Several wooden shelves held pots of old paint and jars filled with rusting bolts and screws.

Nero placed his tools and other items down by the front wheels of the Audi and popped his head underneath, facing upwards. He located the brake pipe, took out his spanner and started to loosen the hose. As the connector came loose, brake fluid began spilling out. Quickly Nero pinched the ends together, taking a small cloth to wipe up the liquid. Then he reattached the pipe with electrical tape. This would keep the brakes working initially, without immediately alerting the driver with a loose brake pedal before the inevitable failure.

Next, he got up and opened the driver door, slid inside and put the vehicle into gear. Back underneath he located the primary handbrake cable. He straightened and pulled out the split pin with pliers, then pushed out the clevis pin with a screwdriver. With a firm yank, the cable came free of the handbrake lever.

Now the handbrake would fail also.

Quickly and silently, Nero cleaned up the scene, packing away his tools into a sports bag and erasing any signs of his deed before slipping back out and returning to his guest house.

Inside, Nero closed the door behind him and paused, glancing around the small studio apartment where Rhodes had housed him. He cleared it of all his belongings and took the small training bag of gear he'd used for the car "adjustments" and the gym bag given to him outside the store. In it was a Walther P99 pistol with 9×19mm Parabellum rounds, new travel documents, ID cards as well as bundles of cash in different currencies.

He changed his clothing and cleaned up the guesthouse, removing any sign that someone had stayed there; folding up the bedsheets and pillowcases and bagging them to take away. He had been there too long for a thorough clean up, but fewer questions would be asked if it looked unoccupied. It was highly unlikely the Colombian police would carry out a forensic sweep of the property following a car crash involving a gringo. Most likely they'd file a report and follow the standard procedures related to automobile accidents; if they even bothered at all.

Nero wiped down the taps, door handles and surfaces anyway, then left with the bags and placed them in the boot of his hire car. He drove out along the curving track and pulled off the road in behind a patch of trees on a piece of scrubland. He had already carried out reconnaissance of the area earlier and pinpointed it as a hidden spot to watch the track entrance to Rhode's place.

Nero checked his watch. 5.30 A.M.

Even on a Sunday, routine in the Rhodes household usually kicked off around seven, so he estimated he'd have enough time to get into position to monitor and follow to check it all went smoothly. Then he waited, as the dawn broke.

Rhodes and his guards would expect Nero's vehicle to have gone that early as he'd already mentioned wanting to go for a morning hike knowing full well that Rhodes had other commitments and wouldn't join him.

Just after 7.30 the white Audi appeared and headed up the hill on his usual routine drive to visit his wife and boy. Troy, his five-year-old son, went to a playgroup with other local kids.

Nero pulled out and followed at a distance.

The route had been studied by Nero closely, explicitly looking for brake points or areas where the vehicle would be at maximum danger. The snaking roads led to a long, steep decline and a high probability of a fatal crash once the speed built after they reached the hill. From his observations Nero had noted that one of Rhodes' Colombian guards who drove, didn't exactly hold back on the gas.

Rhode's vehicle sped up the hill, around the bends that hugged the lush green hills. There was no way of estimating how soon the brake pipe would fail but the car continued up to the crest of the mountain and the descent beyond. Nero increased his speed to keep them in sight.

He needed visual confirmation of the accident, the kill.

The Audi turned out of sight. As it was the weekend, there was no heavy traffic. Their car was descending now, picking up speed. Nero reached the crest, checking his speedometer. They were reaching 120kph. The hazard lights came on, followed by a blaring horn.

The Audi overtook a slower van, narrowly missing an oncoming truck as it increased speed. It disappeared around another bend. When Nero had rounded the corner, the Audi weaved into the middle of the road and at the sight of an oncoming truck overcompensated by swerving too far.

There was a loud crunching bang as the Audi careened along a house wall, then smashed into a stationary car, spinning on impact. It flipped over onto its roof and slid to a standstill. The whole incident was over in less than ten seconds.

Nero reached the accident scene and pulled to a halt. He knew he had to act quickly. They were in an area with a few houses alongside the road. He saw the truck in the rear view slow, then stop, having seen the accident.

Nero grabbed his bag and ran to the upturned Audi. He bent down and peered through a cracked window.

Where the hell was Rhodes?

Just the two of his guards. Both were unconscious but alive.

Nero pulled out a small pack and a hammer. He broke in the window on one side and glanced up the hill. The driver, in a straw cowboy style hat, had jumped down from his cab and looked down at the scene. Nero pulled out a small zip-up bag and took out a syringe filled with potassium chloride and saline water solution; fatal for the heart. He jabbed it into the driver's neck and injected. Then he moved around the other side and carried out the same process. The driver was walking down at a fast pace but not running. Once the injections kicked in, both men would be dead. Any post-mortem would show heart failure for both of them. Not perfect, but it would have to do.

Nero would need to move fast.

He stood up and waved at the driver who was a few metres away.

"I think they're both dead. I'll go and get help," Nero shouted in Spanish. The truck driver looked shocked. He nodded and stared at the smoking vehicle. He knew the driver would likely disappear when Nero had left. Hanging around at a car accident for the policia to come and interrogate you was not a wise move in Colombia.

Nero jumped back into his car, turned it around and headed back towards the *finca* to go hunt down Rhodes.

***

Frank was running along across the main road, beelining for a gas station with a garage set just behind it as he held the phone to his ear, willing Rhodes to pick up.

Shit!

Rhodes still wasn't picking up. The call went to answer message again.

"John! Call me when you get this. Be wary of Nero. I've got good intel he may be out to harm you."

Frank hung up and arrived at the garage, walking up to one of the young mechanics.

"You have a car I can rent?" he asked quickly, in Spanish. The mechanic pointed to an older man standing by a VW Beetle with its rear boot open.

"My boss can help you."

Frank asked the boss the same question who glanced and gestured at a light blue Ford Aspire.

Frank looked at him with an expression of pain.

"Nothing faster?"

Twenty minutes Frank was heading as fast as the Aspire would go, back up through Envigado into the steep hills that towered overhead.

Chapter 38

Earlier that morning, John Rhodes showered, poured himself a coffee and noticed he was low on milk, not to mention bread and other basics. He made a mental note to call the García brothers before sitting down in front of his laptop on the kitchen table. The large windows overlooked the valley of Medellín, and he watched a small bi-plane come in from the east, appearing momentarily through the darkening clouds before it descended over the city towards Olaya Herrera Airport. His plan to take his young son, Troy, to the playgroup had to be aborted after a sleepless night of feverish hell. Whether it was a virus or from too much exertion, he wasn't sure, but it was bad enough for him to have to call off his plans. Instead, he had sent the García brothers to collect his wife, Evelyn, and Troy.

He picked up his mobile phone to call Santiago, one of the brothers. Those men had been reliable and dependable after Rhodes had disappeared into the mists of South America after the Pandora Red episode. A new start for his family and, thanks to help from his increasingly wealthy brother, Michael, a good set-up on the outskirts of Medellín.

The family home was separate for a reason. Close but far enough apart to keep his family out of harm's way, at least in theory. All his intelligence business took place at the finka. The comings and goings of his contacts or in the case of his recent coup, Nero, a place for them to work in safety, out of range from the ears and eyes of potential enemies.

Through his network he had befriended an old Colombian family who had children at Troy's school. They had, like many other Colombians in Medellín, been brought up under the reign of Pablo Escobar. They were tough but smart and just wanted to make the best of their lives. Rhodes had offered two of the brothers, Santiago and Diego, the work of guarding him and keeping him safe. Rhodes knew enemies could always be potentially within reach.

The call connected.

"Santiago?"

"Señor Rhodes? We're just on our way."

"*Hola!* It's OK. I just called to check if you can buy some milk and bread on the way back?"

"Sure, no problem—"

There was a pause and a shout in the background.

"What's happening?"

"The car has no brakes! They don't work at all. I don't know if we can—"

There was a blaring horn in the background. More indistinguishable shouts.

"*¡Cuidado! el camión!*"

Rhodes could only listen in horror as they narrowly missed a truck.

"Santiago?" he shouted. No response.

There was a loud clunk as if the phone dropped onto the floor of the car. More muffled sounds and shouts.

"*El freno de mano está muerto!*"

Then a sound of screeching tyres, a loud bang and the line cut off.

Rhodes re-dialled the number with shaking fingers. A sickening feeling rolled in his stomach. They had crashed, no doubt.

No connection.

Rhodes hauled himself out of his chair to go and get dressed. He'd need to call a taxi. Go find them. The feeling of fever was pushed well out of his mind by concern for the brothers. As he went to his phone to call their family to go and see, it rang in his hand.

Unrecognised number.

Tempted to cut it off, Rhodes then decided otherwise and answered.

"*Hola!*"

"John. It's Mr Milligan."

Rhodes was relieved. It was Frank!

"Hey, I thought you were on a flight? Listen, something terrible has happened to Santiago and Diego. They were in a car accident. I just heard it while speaking to them."

"Why? What happened exactly?"

"I don't know; something about the brakes not working. Then I heard a loud crash."

"Alright, listen to me very carefully. I'm almost certain Nero is a Trojan horse. I spoke to Paterson. He found something; Nero is on a deeper mission to take you out!"

"What?"

Rhodes felt a rush of fear. Not only had he been tricked, but he'd also almost trusted Nero enough to let him in the whole way to their network.

"Are you sure?"

"I'm pretty sure. And now this accident."

"Then the car brakes?"

"Were meant for you. Probably. Were you supposed to be in that car?"

"I. Shit, yes, yes, I was," Rhodes replied.

"Right. Is he there at the finca?"

Rhodes shook his head. "No, no. He left. I saw him leave."

"Thank God! Right, as soon as he realises you're not in the car, he'll come back. You need to hide, get out of there. I'm on my way, but it's another forty minutes from here."

"Right, right," Rhodes started to look around, his mind racing. If he phoned the García family, they might be put at risk. He didn't want Nero rolling in and killing any more of his people.

"Goddammit!" he shouted, his fear forgotten, anger and frustration rising. The deeper he went, the more scumbags came out of the woodwork. Still, it only served to focus his resolve.

Always had.

He went to the window and looked up the driveway. It was quiet but too risky to head up that way. He needed to make for the hills.

"Alright, Frank. I'm going to take off into the hills to the north."

"I need to meet you somewhere. I need location!" Frank barked, the line breaking up.

Rhodes thought for a moment.

"OK, at *La Catedral* prison. It's on the map. There's a road that goes up to it, but I can reach it through a track in the hills."

"Alright. Do you have a weapon?"

"Yes, yes. I can get one, but—"

"OK, get it and move fast and I'll meet you there. Be careful, John!"

Chapter 39

Nero parked in his previous spot, behind the trees and scrubland opposite the track that led to Rhode's farmhouse. He took his bag and weapon, then walked toward the gates.

Had Rhodes been alerted or not?

It was possible he'd somehow heard of the crash and become suspicious. Nero cursed himself for his mistake. He should have put himself in a place where he could see who was actually inside the vehicle before following and wasting all that time.

It didn't matter anyhow. He would find the old man and finish the job. At least those brothers guarding him were out of the way.

Nero came to the gates and wall that sectioned off the property. He scaled the wall with relative ease, then looked around inside. The main house was seemingly devoid of life and the guest house that Nero had stayed in was also quiet.

He jumped down on the far side and remained in a half crouch, looking around before heading to the main building and checking the door. It was locked. He edged around the house, peering through any gaps in the blinds and curtains.

No sign.

Nero took out his pistol, went back to the door and smashed the butt of his gun through the glass, breaking it with a sharp crack. He reached in to unlock the door from the inside, then slowly pushed it open, across the shards of glass on the floor. Nero moved into the corridor, weapon now poised.

He edged into the kitchen, a smell of coffee still lingering and spotted the source; a mug and coffee pot on the kitchen table. He doubled back and checked the living room and the back room that served as the computer centre.

Creeping up the stairs, he kept his weapon aimed directly in front of him and edged around the corners, confirming each of the bedrooms and bathroom were empty.

Rhodes was gone.

Had he been alerted? Taken off somewhere? His guards had taken his only car. Unless he had been picked up by someone? The timeline from the guards leaving, the crash and Nero returning was just over an hour. If he had been picked up, that would mean he'd have arranged it pretty quickly, even if he did know about the accident. No, it seemed more likely Rhodes had left on foot. He was a keen hiker and knew the various tracks around the forests reasonably well, but if he needed somewhere to hide, where would he go?

Nero left the house and checked the guest house where he had been staying. All clean and empty as he had left it.

La Catedral? It was within walking distance. Not easy through those rocky paths but an option. Had he overheard Rhodes mention it to Frank at some point?

Nero was undecided.

Track him on foot or—

He moved across the manicured lawn and let himself into the garage. The motorbike was still under the sheet. After rummaging around for a few minutes, he located the keys hanging up and set about getting it started.

***

Rhodes walked hastily along the rocky path, coming to a fast-moving stream with dispersed rocks that he carefully navigated across. He had run into the nearby forest. Heading to the road risked coming face to face with Nero coming the other way. Much easier to hide in amongst the natural chaos. His plan, in this panicked last-minute dash away from danger, was to head to the beginnings of another road across the hills, around twelve kilometres away. He'd done it before, in about three hours, then he would call Frank from the mobile he'd taken.

After that, God only knows, thought Rhodes. He had been badly exposed. All his precautions had counted for nothing. A Trojan horse, an enemy of the most dangerous kind. Rhodes had spent the entire previous year setting up his hideaway and taking every precaution he knew to keep his whereabouts secret. The new identity, with all the corresponding fake information required to make it credible. But they had found him, through his own idiotic stupidity.

Lessons would have to be learned. If he ever survived this.

Then a horrifying thought came to him. His family at the other house. Maybe Nero wasn't even going to try to return to find him? Perhaps somehow he had found out the secret of his wife and son's location.

He had to move faster. But it would be hours before he got in any position to do anything. He tried his phone again, but the signal was weak and cut out intermittently.

Should he turn back and return to the finca? Try and flag down a car or phone Frank to change the plan or call the García family for help?

Rhodes stopped and took a swig from the water bottle he'd hurriedly snatched before wiping his brow, glancing down at the stream behind him. He decided against it. Getting back and then to the main road would take just as long.

Goddamnit!!

He moved off again at a half-jog as his journey became more urgent, panting loudly as the path became steeper, lined with hazardous tree roots and rocks jutting out of the dry soil. In his haste a loose rock dislodged his foot and a sharp pain shot through his ankle.

Shit!

He stumbled, then stopped, leaning over with his hands on his legs, panting. He wanted to shout out in pain, in frustration, but the risk of giving away his location stopped him dead.

"Well done, John. Well done, mate," he muttered under his breath before hobbling on up the path.

***

When he finally got onto the home run within five kilometres of the RV point, Frank tried calling Rhodes again but couldn't get through at all. He would have to trust that Rhodes could make it on his own. His wasn't exactly a young man, Frank thought. He followed narrow, steep roads for several kilometres, then came to a junction that had two houses and some shack-turned-bar that overlooked Medellín. Frank asked a local woman for directions and then continued up the winding *Caldra–Envigado* road until he found the gates of the old prison, *La Catedral*.

He parked outside, got out of his car and looked around. It was quiet.

He moved inside the gates that had been wrenched open, walked down a slope towards a half-sized concrete football pitch with small goalposts and nets where Pablo Escobar had invited the Colombian football team to play with him. There were remnants of furnishings scattered over the ground; a smashed china sink, taps, tiles that appeared to have been stripped and carried out. Overlooking the pitch on his left side were small buildings with steps leading up to a terrace wall, the windows smashed.

He crept along the wall and moved up the steps until he was on a terrace. He peeked through one of the building windows. There had been a large living quarters here, with remnants of the luxury that Escobar had once lived in, stripped since his death.

Frank checked around the back of the building and then returned to the terrace. From that spot he could see an old helicopter pad set lower down the hill, beyond it the golden hills spreading outwards towards another panoramic view of the Envigado enclave of Medellín, partly obscured by a mist that had begun to rise.

There was no sign of Rhodes. How long could Frank wait here?

Frank headed back down to the football pitch, along a walkway with other single-level buildings; all empty and trashed. He passed narrow steps leading down to the helipad and continued on round, past an old guard tower to a wide track that led into the jungle.

That would be the direction Rhodes would come.

Frank walked down the path, thick with trees on one side, the same expansive view of the golden hills as from the helipad on the other.

Frank half jogged down the track until it narrowed and split; the path heading down a slope would be the route Rhodes would come.

After around ten minutes Frank heard a rustling noise ahead and hid behind a nearby line of rocks and waited.

A distinct footfall, slow and lumbering, came nearer. It was Rhodes, holding a makeshift staff, limping.

Frank stepped out to show himself. Rhodes' face turned from surprise to relief.

"Thank God!"

Frank went over, checking his leg.

"Are you hurt?"

"Ah, just slipped and twisted the old ankle, it's slowed me down a bit, but he's back there somewhere, Frank. I know he is."

Frank took a look down the track, then back up to the way he had come.

"Alright, we'd better get moving as fast as we can." He went to help Rhodes, but the older man waved his stick ahead. "I'll be alright. Just keep eyes behind."

"Did you get a weapon?" Frank asked.

"Yeah, I got it." He held out a Glock 17 for Frank to take.

"Good. I think we're going to need it."

Chapter 40

As they approached *La Catedral*, the dark silhouette of the old guard tower loomed against a swirling grey sky. Heavy raindrops began to fall, splattering against the plants and ground before slowly turning to a steady cascade that soaked them both to the skin.

They moved onto the concrete path towards the first row of buildings. Frank had been keeping most of his focus behind but now had to be wary of what lay in the old prison grounds. Squinting from the raindrops running down into his eyes, Frank moved cautiously, aiming the Glock ahead at potential ambush points as they edged forward. He signalled Rhodes to stay close.

The first doorway led into a small space which looked like it had been a chapel, the remnants of wooden pews covered in dust and a stone statue of the Virgin Mary on a small altar. The roof had partially collapsed, and the rain now formed pools of water on the floor. Frank moved into the vestry, a small confined space at the back. He carefully opened another door and saw it led to the other side of the building.

They moved on, Frank methodically checking each potential hiding space.

The further they went in, past broken windows and dozens of blind spots, the more he realised it was looking like a turkey shoot. He didn't like it.

The pounding rain disguised their footfall at least, thought Frank.

But it also would mask Nero's. The more rooms and buildings Frank cleared, the more his senses told him Nero was playing ghosts.

Rhodes' limp seemed to be getting worse. If they were in a situation where moving fast was required, it would be over. And, as Frank knew only too well, being stationary or slow heightened the chances of being killed.

Got to keep moving.

Rhodes limped ahead and Frank turned to check their rear; a gap on his right revealed the steps leading up to other buildings further up the hill. A light thud sound cut through the rain. Frank turned to see Rhodes had slipped down onto the pathway by a door.

Another thud.

Gunfire.

Frank dived to the ground.

Where was it coming from?

He belly-crawled over to Rhodes, who had frozen in place.

"It's him." Frank gestured with his hand. Rhodes began crawling back to Frank and the gap between the two buildings.

"Where is he?" Rhodes rasped. Frank glimpsed around the corner where Rhodes had slipped for any clue, then turned back.

"I think he's up in those buildings." Frank jerked his head in the direction of the single-storey buildings up the hill, out of sight from their position.

Rhodes propped himself up against the wall; pain etched on his face.

Frank wondered briefly why the hell he had to hurt his ankle at a time like this but kept his mouth shut. The only thing to do was for Rhodes to hole up somewhere while he hunted down Nero. He looked around and remembered the first building. The chapel.

"Alright, let's retrace our steps."

They headed back, knowing Nero was up in the higher buildings enabled them to move as fast as they could with Rhode's swollen ankle.

Back inside, Frank had another look around. Alongside the pews was an old wooden table on its side and sheets of corrugated metal resting against the wall.

"Hide somewhere so you can see this doorway and window." He pointed at the space they had come through. There's another exit if you need it. I wish we had two weapons—"

Rhodes eased himself down on a pew. "He could've killed me at any time," Rhodes muttered.

"He needed it to be an accident, but I'm not sure he'll care, now." Frank was looking through an arched doorway to another space next to the altar. "Think Escobar prayed here, John?" Rhodes snorted as if he couldn't care less.

Frank gestured to him. "Alright, in here. Quick!"

Rhodes hobbled inside.

"You can see the door and window from here." Frank was standing at the doorway. "And there's an escape route." He pointed at another doorless space that led to the opposite side at the back then walked out into the main area. Rhodes followed him out as Frank pulled up the old table and quietly shifted it along to the doorway, leaning it upright to act as a block to that entrance. Then he grabbed the few concrete blocks on the ground and placed them against the underside of the table, while Rhodes took the corrugated iron, adding to the barricade.

"Won't last too long, but it'll buy you a few precious seconds."

"Keep an eye on both. He could come either way."

"So you're taking off on holiday?"

Frank checked his Glock. "Yeah, hear it's better food down south." He patted Rhodes on the shoulder and caught his eye, face deadly serious.

"I'm going to get him. If anything happens to me, you've got a clear run back into the woods. Just stay hidden and don't make a sound. We'll go with 'high' and 'five' to identify each other. Is that clear?

Rhodes nodded. "High—"

"Five," Frank finished.

"Thanks, Frank."

"Thank me when this shit storm is over."

Frank moved back outside via the more hidden rear exit, assuming a firing position as he headed along the exterior wall. At a gap between the buildings, he switched back to the main path, continuing in the same direction. The rain was coming down in torrential waves now. Frank duck-walked along the edge of the building back to their previous position within sight of the steps leading up the hill directly ahead. He carefully edged a quick look around the corner, but the visibility was almost zero. Nero must have the steps covered. It would be suicidal to take that route – had to find another way.

On the wooden door frame where Rhodes had slipped and narrowly avoided being shot, Frank saw the bullet holes. He was or had been on their left flank, up in the buildings that hung overhead, looking down on them from the hill and Medellín beyond.

Frank, half-crouched, moved around the building, back towards the path from the forest they had come through. He then cut back toward the prison grounds and headed back through the trees, up to a hill towards the buildings. He kept his eyes peeled ahead, glancing down at the ground to see if there were any tracks left by Nero.

What the hell had happened? How had he got ahead?

He shook the questions from his mind, treading through the under-growth as he ascended the hill, pistol aimed ahead. The rain had begun to ease, the distant roar fading as Frank reached the peak to face the old red brick building that had once 'imprisoned' the most famous narco in the world. He edged his way to the rear, as far back as he could go before a mound of rock formed a sheer cliff reaching into the grey sky.

With his pistol continuously covering the edges of each wall against potential fire, Frank traversed and secured most of the east side but inside the buildings was another matter. Down to his right, he could see the single-storey blocks, with the church building at the end, where Rhodes was hopefully still hiding. Beyond the wall, steps and helipad lay the Colombian panorama, its vibrant green vista dulled by the dying rain.

Suddenly, a bullet whistled past him; the concentration of his effort shattered. He dropped fast and took a glance along the line. An exposed window, and a flicker of movement. Frank fired a burst, then leapt forward, closing the space to a pile of rubble and fell behind it. After a few seconds he rummaged around and grabbed a clump of loose concrete.

With a quick flick of the arm, he tossed it at the roof of the building. The concrete crashed into the tiles, causing a cascade of movement. Frank jumped to his feet, covering the final few metres to reach the wall of the second building next to the window, and slammed against it. He peered over the sill of the window and through the space of the glassless frame with the barrel of the Glock scanning the inside. A distant noise of shifting rubble caught his attention. Frank knew Nero had moved on and was no longer in the room. He opened the rusty window and proceeded to take a good look inside to check before hauling himself through.

Inside, Frank barely noticed the large, spacious area had been stripped of anything of value. He aimed his barrel and edged forward to a pair of double doors at the far end. Beyond, the floors caught the light from some unseen window. The rain had completely stopped now, leaving Frank feeling naked and exposed from the lack of covering noise.

He carefully moved forward to the side of the doors, lowered himself to his haunches and listened for any hint of Nero's position. However, all he could hear was the distant sound of birdsong from the surrounding trees. Frank edged his barrel around the doorframe into another space, a smashed-in window on the far wall revealing itself as the source of the exterior sounds and an upturned table.

Frank checked his arc of fire, left, right then moved inside in short sprints to the table, then swiftly moved again to the exterior window.

No sign. Frank began to worry.

He looked down to the church and decided to head back. There was a sudden bang, like wood hitting the ground punctured the air from the direction of the church.

Rhodes!

Frank descended quickly down the steps to the lower buildings in a trot. He moved along the bottom of the hill towards the rear of the church, then cut through a side alley to the main path.

Another crunch, a shifting of wood as if the barricade was being ripped apart.

The bastard had outmanoeuvred him.

Running at full pelt now, Frank caught sight of Nero as he climbed through the doorway of the church. Too late for a shot.

As he reached the exterior of the church wall, Frank slowed to a halt, crouched low just by the doorway. The barricade had been breached. The table top was shoved aside.

If Rhodes was still in there, he was dead.

With a sharp exhale, Frank swung his aim inside. He saw a glimpse of Nero's black shirt as he moved through the interior doorway of the vestry and fired a shot, bursting open a cloud of debris on the stone wall. He didn't hesitate and moved fast, straight to the wall he'd just shot. A light scrape sounded outside the rear door through the vestry.

With another swift move Frank stepped into the vestry room where Rhodes should have been hiding.

Except he wasn't.

Must have run out the back and now Nero is right on him.

Frank was about to go out after them but decided to go back to the front and pincer Nero. When he got to the door, he saw Nero crouched by the bottom of the guard tower aiming in his direction. He jumped back just as a bullet whizzed past the door.

He crouched low, pointed a blind aim and fired back in his general direction, then moved back inside and looked up to the collapsed ceiling leading to the roof.

Low enough.

He tucked his Glock into his belt, stepped onto the table that had been shoved aside, grabbed the exposed metal joists and hauled himself up with both arms. With a swing of the legs he was quickly on top of the chapel flat roof. He retrieved his pistol, got down on his front and crawled along to a decorated parapet with holes on the edge

Nero had moved to the right side of the tower, anticipating Frank to come at him from the rear of the chapel, then he glanced back down into the woods behind him, where Rhodes must have headed. Nero moved his focus back onto the chapel.

He apparently wanted to deal with Frank first.

Frank aimed for his body mass, taking his time, and squeezed the trigger. Yet Nero moved just as the hammer fell and the shot missed by a fraction but the bullet still caught the top of Nero's thigh, sending him reeling and stumbling to the ground.

There's another nice flesh wound for you, mate.

Alerted to Frank's new position, Nero returned a shot but it was way off, then he rolled across the ground in an attempt to hide. Frank fired again, hitting the metal skeleton of the guard tower.

Peeping through the parapet holes, Frank saw Nero hobbling away in the direction of the jungle path.

Run, you bastard, run.

Frank stood up, then leapt down the twelve feet or so to the ground, landing on his haunches. He scurried in a half crouch over to the tower, then sighted on Nero just as he crawled into a wall of the jungle behind a group of trees. Frank jogged to the edge of the trees on the same side, melting into the foliage, then set about stalking his wounded prey.

Step by step, he inched closer, gaining on his target fast. He caught glimpses of Nero moving away from him, just a few steps ahead now. Through a gap in the trees, Frank saw space in the vegetation and ran hard, then dived, tackling Nero around the waist with one arm and grabbing his pistol arm with the other. Both men hit the muddy ground with a jolt and a shout of pain.

Nero tried to roll Frank off, but his free arm was being jerked behind his back with lightning speed. Frank adjusted his stance and planted a knee onto his lower spine. Another grunt of pain.

"Release your weapon."

There was a pause, then Nero slowly loosened his grip on the pistol.

Just then, Frank heard a noise and looked up to see Rhodes appear through a cluster of jungle plants.

"Grab his gun!" Frank rasped.

Rhodes did so and pointed it down at their new prisoner. Frank rolled off, stood up and pulled out his pistol to train on Nero. Rhodes stepped forward and booted Nero in the waist.

"Aaargh!"

"You fucking killed my friends, you little shit!" Rhodes' voice was full of venom. He looked across at Frank. "Let's just kill him and leave him here with all the other ghosts."

He looked like he meant it.

Frank ignored him and jerked his pistol at Nero. "Get on your hands and knees." Then, to Rhodes, "keep an eye on him, I gotta search him." A patch of dark red was spreading through his combat trousers. "And check that wound."

Frank found no other weapons or knives and allowed Nero to bandage his wound with a piece of ripped shirt. Nero looked up and offered Frank a thin smile. "So, you decided to come back, huh, mate?"

"Just for you. We figured out your game, Nero or whoever the fuck you are. Is it CIA?"

"Does it matter? You think any intelligence agency would tolerate an organisation like G13COMM coming into existence?"

"Screwed up all your plans?"

Nero sneered. "Not mine. I don't personally give a flying fuck." His breathing quickened, spitting out the words, his face winching from pain, "The big sharks upstairs care though; a lot. I do the work required; used to be terrorists but I guess we're in a new era and some cleaning up phase; pinpointing internal enemies."

"You mean like my organisation? Publishing news you don't like?" said Rhodes, with contempt.

"Bullshit news and building whatever the hell the network is you're building with your survivalist buddies, Mr Rhodes?"

"I guess being candid with the truth would be beyond the pale for the likes of your type."

Nero flashed him a look of disdain.

"Let's go!" said Frank, levelling the weapon at Nero. He struggled to his feet and they walked slowly through to a small football field, Nero ahead with his hands raised, Frank behind while Rhodes stayed back. Frank turned his head. "John, you OK to drive? I don't want to give him any chances."

"Yes, I can drive. What are we doing with him?" Rhodes whispered.

It was a good point. Frank was now swimming in an unknown sea. Could he get Carl to help? He had a double agent on his hands, as well as effectively being one himself. His employers would want him back and what would happen to Frank or Rhodes?

Nero was now a few more steps ahead.

"Do you think your place is safe?" It was a rhetorical question. It was impossible to know. Certainly, Nero must have had plenty of chances while staying to update his employers on his location.

"No, but I know where we can take him until we get this sorted out," Rhodes replied.

They reached the car. "In the front," Frank ordered Nero. Frank quickly slipped into the rear seat just behind him, while Rhodes eased himself into the driver seat.

They headed back to the winding road, past sporadic houses that were perfectly positioned for views across the valley. Glimpses of Medellín appeared through the rain clouds that moved overhead. The narrow road widened until they came to the main route back to the city, joining the main flow of traffic. They drove in silence, the sound of pattering rain and the squeaking wipers frantically clearing an arched view through the windscreen that was steaming up.

Rhodes wound down his window halfway and rubbed a circle of condensation away from the screen. As they gathered speed, Nero suddenly pulled the handbrake, causing a screech of the tyres and the vehicle to slide at an angle on the wet Tarmac.

"What the—" Rhodes shouted, struggling to control the vehicle as it nearly collided with oncoming traffic.

Simultaneously, Nero slammed his seat back against Frank, pinning his legs, then half turned to grab Frank's wrist with the pistol pulling Frank forward while twisting his arm.

Rhodes slammed the brakes, too hard, sending the car careering across the road. It skidded side on against the flow of oncoming traffic. A speeding vehicle clipped the rear end of their Ford Aspire, sending it spinning until it hit a concrete post on the edge of the road with a loud crack.

The gun flew out of Frank's hand, bouncing off the edge of the passenger window, then out onto the road. He cracked his forehead on the seat in front and fell back dazed.

Through his confusion, he sensed the passenger door open. Rhodes lunged for Nero and missed. Frank saw the shadow of Nero move across the rain-washed window, then the weapon rose, pointing at Rhodes.

With all the strength he could summon, he slammed open the door hard against Nero who fell back onto the road but managed to keep on his feet. Frank began moving out of the car and saw Nero steady himself, raising the pistol toward his head.

A loud horn, screeching like the bellowing of frenzied cattle.

Nero turned to see the oncoming truck, but it was too late. His body fell under the huge engine grill and wheels with a dull thud as if mown down by a freight train.

The truck wheels screamed as the brakes locked, sending it turning across the road.

Another loud collision of metal as another car narrowly avoided crashing into it, only to careen into the vehicle in front.

The truck continued braking with a piercing screech until it came to a halt in a cloud of smoke.

Frank looked back at the road in front of him, the crumpled, bloody corpse of Nero lay twisted across the wet Tarmac.

"Jesus!"

Both ends of the road now had stationary cars that had come to an abrupt halt.

Frank leaned down, peering into the car.

"John! You ok, mate?"

Rhodes peered across at the carnage in the road, his face frozen in shock.

"We've gotta get out of here. Head to your friend's place on foot," Frank said, loud and clear.

Rhodes continued to stare at him, still seemingly paralysed.

"Come on, John. Move!"

The shout cut through, stirring him into action and he pushed open his door and clambered out of the car.

They moved across the road and Frank leaned down over Nero, his breathing shallow as he searched the wet red pockets.

"Wish it could've been so different, mate," he whispered.

He felt something and pulled out a USB flash drive.

"Thought so," he said, quietly.

"Come on!" It was John, by the side of the road, now fully alert to the risk of hanging around.

Frank jogged over and they both disappeared into the trees, away from the honking horns and growing sound of distant sirens.

Chapter 41

Frank, Rhodes and the García brothers' mother and father were sitting at a table, littered with coffee mugs, ashtrays and a bottle of Aguardiente, on the veranda of their house looking out across acres of farmland. Two chestnut horses grazed nearby. An idyllic scene in direct contrast with what Frank and Rhodes had been through hours before.

The mother broke out into sporadic tears as the father fought his grief with continuous coffee, booze and cigarettes, his face fixed with shell shock. They had only recently heard of their sons' deaths in a terrible car accident.

A young boy, no older than five, played with his trucks on the living room floor, oblivious to the grief that cast gloom over the household.

Rhodes leaned forward clasping his hands together, his own shock from earlier events erased by concern for them, and offered words of comfort. Their daughter, early twenties with jet black hair and light skin, looked equally forlorn as she bandaged Frank's forehead, then proceeded to check his other scrapes and bruises.

"*Gracias*," he kept saying, unsure of how to console her.

The father's phone rang, and he spoke for a few moments in Spanish before ending the call.

"My sons are at the morgue. I need to go and make arrangements. Please make yourselves at home." He looked over at his daughter. "Valentina will make up the guest room if you need it."

"Thank you, Mateo. We won't stay long," John said, gratefully.

"Stay as long as you like, but get your wife and kid here. It'll be safer," Mateo added. He patted John on the shoulder. "Please be our guests. You were very kind to our sons. And the man responsible is dead, yes?"

"Yes, he certainly is."

The father nodded, his expression becoming cold as stone. "*Muy Bien.*"

***

Later in the evening Frank and Rhodes found themselves alone on the veranda as the evening closed in, sipping on their drinks. The rain had long dispersed as the sun set behind the far lush green hills.

"So what have we got?" Frank asked.

"Two good men dead. I hoped it wouldn't come to this."

Frank shuffled in his chair and nodded. "I still can't believe Nero—"

"His story was watertight. None of us could have seen that coming. I screwed up and nearly compromised the whole of Liberatus. What a mess." Rhodes shook his head and drained his glass.

Frank reached into his pocket and handed over the flash drive he had taken from Nero on the road.

"Before I forget. This is probably Liberatus data he was trying to steal."

Rhodes took it. "Thanks, Frank. That was fast thinking."

Frank leaned back, observing Rhodes with relief. "Well, you're still alive, thank God. You believe that he was CIA?"

"Certainly not officially sanctioned, that's for sure. But it makes sense. It has to be a small unit deep inside, operating without any remit to the official hierarchy," Rhodes mused.

"As bad as G13COMM, huh?" Frank said, laughing without humour.

"They fucking deserve each other. If they were out to protect the citizens, well, I wouldn't hate them so much. After all, I was MI6 once. But they're not. They serve their own interests, the military–industrial complex and that of their masters. They are run by psychopaths." Rhodes leaned over to the bottle of Aguardiente, offered Frank another who declined, and poured himself another one.

"I'm sure they have good people too."

"I'm sure." Rhodes snorted, "Well, the red dots will be circling our heads soon enough. We'll both need to lie low," Rhodes added, ominously.

Frank sighed. "So, I need to look over my shoulder."

"You'll be alright. Nero is dead. That female assassin is dead. You're a formidable force to be reckoned with. Your legends were solid from my end, but I can't vouch for Carl, of course."

Frank studied his empty glass. Another loose end he'd need to tie up. Still, he'd done what Paterson had wanted. Turned Nero into roadkill on the Tarmac. The vision of the carnage on the road flashed into his mind and he reached for the bottle.

"And the paramilitaries we came against, in the pay of G13COMM, no doubt."

"Can't be certain, but it makes sense. They wanted Nero dead for all the milk he was about to spill."

"You have all the data he gave you secured?"

Rhodes smiled. "Don't worry, Frank. I know what I'm doing on that front. Yes, it's secure. I made a call to get the farm thoroughly 'cleaned'." He glanced at his watch. "Should be nearly done."

"What are you going to do with it? The data, I mean?"

"Well, I'm going to be very careful right now, Frank. Very careful indeed." Rhodes sucked in air through his teeth. "Right now, it's leverage, that's all. But, if needed, it might serve a purpose."

"Hmm, very cryptic, John."

"What now?" Frank asked, sipping on the anise-flavoured liqueur.

Rhodes sighed and leaned back in his recliner, staring out at the misty haze.

"Well, it's over. I'll get your last payment organised, as arranged." He turned to look at Frank. "The car. We left it at the scene."

"Yeah, don't worry. I hired it under the alias you gave me. It'll lead nowhere, so I'll need a new one if you can arrange it?"

Rhodes nodded.

"I could use the one Carl gave me, but it might be a risk," added Frank.

Rhodes shook his head. "No, don't risk it. You don't know if it's compromised or what the bloody hell is going on between Ghost 13 in the UK and the CIA. Mateo has contacts here. We'll get you sorted out so you can get back home."

"What are you going to do?"

"I'll move on but stay in South America. It's easier to get lost here, stay under the radar."

"Just make sure you do. You're gonna have to be more careful than ever."

John sighed. "I know, I know."

Chapter 42

G13COMM. Colorado air base.

In the series of barren, dark cubicles, illuminated only by the fluorescent ceiling lights, the G13COMM teams working on Operation Darkwood hunched over their desks. Colonel Wexhall walked briskly along the corridor that joined them together, glancing through the glass of each one with a stony glare.

Nero and his handler, whoever the guy was, had slipped his grasp, gotten clean away and he needed to resume the trail. First, his own men had screwed up on the ship. Then the AUC couldn't even deal with them in their own damned jungle.

Wexhall entered his private office and paced around the room. He stared at the blank wall at the back. He should get a big painting up there, a battle scene and a damned glorious one. The phone rang. It was the encrypted internal line.

"Colonel Wexhall? It's Sergeant Major Stark" came the monotone voice. "Sir, I have an update on the field situation," he added.

"Go ahead."

"The one believed to be Nero was found dead outside Medellín. He stepped in front of a truck according to reports picked up on the police network. We're eighty per cent certain it was him."

Wexhall nodded. That was good. A stroke of luck however it happened.

"That's interesting. What about the other guy with him?"

"No sign of him, I'm afraid. Disappeared. But there's something else—"

"Yes, Sergeant Major."

"Nero was almost certainly a CIA agent."

There was a pause. Wexhall stared at the desk, momentarily frozen. That was messy. They had inadvertently been hunting down someone from the company.

Not good.

"We identified him from surveillance cameras on the chopper over the *Anita*. The photo recog only just came up with a ninety per cent match. We also got a match on the fingerprint from his house from our man inside. It's on the CIA database. He's definitely one of theirs—"

The line began beeping, indicating another call.

"I'll get back to you, Sergeant Major." Wexhall looked at the number, then tapped a button on the handset.

A low, husky whisper came over the line; faint but exuding power. A voice Wexhall recognised immediately.

"Wexhall. You know who this is?"

"Yes."

"Good. You need to close down Darkwood immediately, without hesitation."

"I don't understand?"

"There's nothing to question here. It'll have to wait for another day. There is a Senate enquiry about to happen and you'll need to appear and answer questions."

Wexhall sunk into his reclining office chair as if dealt a second body blow. "I don't understand. I thought we had everything covered—"

"We'll deal with that. In the meantime, you need to close down the operation; get rid of everything, and I mean absolutely everything."

The line went dead.

Wexhall slammed the handset down. He grabbed his china mug, filled with coffee, and threw it at the blank wall. The cup smashed, splattering the brown liquid across the paintwork like the blood from a gunshot wound.

CIA Headquarters, Langley

"This has to be Wexhall," said Fallon.

Brett Fallon, Deputy Director for Operations, and Kate Foster, the Deputy Executive Director, were in a small comms room. Fallon was sitting in front of the console while Foster paced, pausing occasionally. The large screen on the wall had the encrypted message lingering on the screen with the confirmation that their field agent had been confirmed dead. The snippets of information from the ground were sparse, the breakdown in intel over the previous few weeks had made the situation on the ground hazy at best. But CIA-backed Colombian sources on the ground had acquired pictures that clearly showed their agent dead in a traffic accident.

"We've lost a good man there. It's unfortunate. But not entirely outside the orbit of our profession," Foster said, in a matter-of-fact tone. "It's likely to have involved Rhodes. We just don't know."

Fallon held the expression of a man unconvinced and stared into the mid-distance.

"It's over, Fallon. Wrap this shit up. For now, our mission is nearly complete. Wexhall will fall, soon."

Chapter 43

"Jesus! You left him spread over the Tarmac?"

"I didn't personally chop him up or anything. It was an accident."

There was a pause as Carl considered. "Ironic, the way things work out considering he was trying to put Rhodes through the accident meat grinder himself."

"I liked him," Frank said, without thinking. "He just had his moral compass in the wrong place. I didn't want to see him die that way," he added, swapping the satellite phone to his other ear. He peered out through the farmhouse window across at the rolling Irish countryside. The briquettes needed bringing in, or the fire would die. It would be a right pain to get going again.

"Friends and enemies. There's an indistinguishable blur between them in our business,"

Tell me about it, thought Frank, his previous friendship with Carl coming into focus.

"So, we're wrapped up then," Frank said, wanting to finish the conversation.

Carl got what he wanted. G13COMM was sunk, and he retained his power base with Ghost 13 in London.

"Essentially. Although you did go off-piste and disobey orders."

"Naturally," Frank cut in.

"Handing over the asset to the wrong crowd. I'll never employ you again. You're talented, Frank, but you're ill-disciplined. I'll need a debrief in London ASAP."

Frank sighed. "Alright. I'll be seeing you, Carl." He cut the line, dropped the phone on a table, and headed outside to fill up a bucket with turf briquettes. He brought them inside and tossed them into the fire in the stove, watching the flames build.

There was some basic furniture still in the house, but he had driven over enough clothes, a sleeping bag, work tools and a small box of possessions to the house once the contracts were exchanged. He stood up and looked around at the walls. Some would need plastering, followed by a lick of paint. It was going to be great to focus on the straightforward work of refurbishing his new house. He was looking forward to it; the therapeutic act of painting, listening to music, switching off his mind to the previous escapades.

A news item on the radio caught his attention, and he went to turn up the volume. A Senate hearing had the spotlight on the intelligence community once again.

"Doug, the big question here is: did any US intelligence agency, CIA or otherwise, have connections with the paramilitary group the United Defence Forces of Colombia? Remember, this is a group that is rumoured to have been involved in numerous massacres, some extremely gruesome incidents involving beheadings as well as the brutal killing of women and children. Colonel Wexhall will be fielding questions from the committee about this."

The news moved on, and Frank switched it off with a wry smile. Perhaps John Rhodes had planted a leak somewhere, stirred the pot; the old man still dealing a strong hand even as he disappeared with his wife and son into the mists of South America.

Frank headed to one of the bags he had brought over and cut open the inside lining where he had stashed a brand-new legend passport, arranged when he had got back to London. He had decided to wrap it up in plastic and tape it behind one of the plasterboards when he redid the inside walls.

At that moment his mobile rang and he fished it out of his pocket, glancing at the display. He smiled seeing Maria's caller ID and answered.

Author's Note

I didn't travel to Colombia in early 2017 to write *Ghost Order*. The story didn't yet exist in my mind but the way it came about dovetailed nicely with my journey at that time.

In December 2016 I had given away or sold most of my possessions, given notice on my day job and with a vague plan to be a travelling nomadic writer for as long as possible, headed to the embarkation point of the Nomad Cruise in Las Palmas, Gran Canaria.

This would be a two-week kick-off party to a plan that was vaguely centred around finding a sun-kissed utopia to write books and possibly freelance on the side. The cruise itself was for Digital Nomads, a creative mix of mostly younger, smart Europeans who made it their business to travel the world and work online. That cruise opened my eyes to the possibilities of the new nomadic lifestyle; one of moving from country to country, enjoying the fruits of each one while edging away from any winter nastiness.

The cruise arrived in the Dominican Republic just before Christmas, and I have to admit not having a great time there. An accident at a lagoon cut open my foot and I had my precious iPhone stolen days later. I was glad to leave.

My trip, followed in Frank's footsteps, was as yet unwritten. To the Caribbean by boat, with stops at Antigua, Barbados, St Martin and St Lucia.

I arrived in Cartagena, Colombia, with a determination to get back on track, with both my mindset and my work, and after a month came to Medellín, the city of eternal spring.

The subsequent trips I took while there, including a trek to the self-built prison of Pablo Escobar, La Catedal, would provide more inspiration. Those who have watched the Netflix series *Narcos* will be familiar with the background to that place. It became the setting of the showdown finale in *Ghost Order*, naturally.

At the time *White Horse* (the first book in the Dark Paradigm series) was with the editor, and I was deep in first draft stage with *Red Horse* (mostly set in Iran). So I was in a different world when it came to my fiction as opposed to my location. The dream is to be writing on location wherever my book is set. One day. But staying in Cartagena, on the Caribbean coast and then Medellín, certainly simmered the imagination, and the seed for *Ghost Order* was sown.

After my return (the digital nomad thing didn't work out!) in October/November 2017, I began piecing together the plot for *Ghost Order* and then saw that authorpreneur Derek Murphy had a spot going at his castle writing retreat in Rappottenstein, Austria. Yes, a sanctuary for writers during NaNoWriMo (National Novel Writing Month). Too good to miss and what a place to get stuck into *Ghost Order*.

So a group of writers spent almost two weeks in this fantastic location: writing, eating, drinking, walking in the surrounding forest, the occasional road trip to other castles and a border run to Czech, then more writing...lots of writing. By the end, I had a very rough first draft and the past year has been honing and reworking the story. It has been great to be working on a Frank Bowen story again after that four-year break.

There is, of course, a wider team behind the story. I also have to thank the beta readers, Diane and Dorene, who have been with me for several years now. James Newton who has spent a lot of his time copy-editing. Collaborative partner Jay Newton who mechanically dismantles the weaknesses and finds the missing parts. Thanks also to Nicky Lovick for the final edit.

So that is the story behind the story. And what next for Frank Bowen? There is undoubtedly a long gap between this latest episode in 2000 until the Dark Paradigm series, where Frank's offspring come into their own in the epic struggle to prevent an apocalypse. Let's see where the inspiration and ideas manifest next, and perhaps I will throw darts at a globe to find out where my and Frank's next destination lies.

Jay Tinsiano

Bristol, United Kingdom

FREE Thriller!

Exclusive offer. To grab your FREE Novella eBook (Blood Tide) head to:
http://jaytinsiano.com/secret-access/

PLUS you'll get access to the VIP Jay Tinsiano reading group for:

- Free Books and stories
- Previews and Sneak Peeks
- Exclusive material

Also Available

White Horse

Half a world away in Spain and running from his past, a Los Angeles gangster unwittingly takes a train that's headed straight into a terrorist attack. He survives only to face an even deadlier threat.

On that same train: a virologist with clues to a deadly epidemic. Did his secrets die with him in the strike?

Raging in the aftermath, a foul-tempered police chief with a daughter caught in the attack thirsts for revenge. But against whom?

An orphan child without a name disappears down a dark, illegal CIA mind-control programme. Now trained in the ways of death, he prepares to do his master's twisted bidding.

From its first pages, the relentless techno-thriller White Horse drops you with a thunderclap in the middle of these colliding worlds. This tale of global conspiracy that threatens humanity itself will keep you guessing whether anyone can survive.

Available at all major eBook retailers
Paperback ISBN: 978-1-9997232-1-7

Red Horse

Haleema Sheraz, a cyber hacker for the Iranian government, discovers her father has gone missing. Frustrated at the lack of urgency from the police, she investigates and soon reveals a kidnapping network that spans back to Operation Paperclip in World War II.

Meanwhile, her brothers join an ISIS-inspired uprising that is wreaking havoc inside Iran, and finding her father quickly becomes a mission to save her family.

Joe Bowen and Hugo Reese continue to prepare Liberatus for a wider global struggle and find themselves called to help one of their own secret assets-Sirus aka Haleema Sheraz.

Soon they will all be thrust into the battle zone and their lives will change irreversibly in this epic story of bitter struggle against the backdrop of total war.

Available at all major eBook retailers
Paperback ISBN: 978-1-9997232-4-8

Flight 313

A group of men board flight 313 with the equipment and means to hijack the aircraft.

An air marshal who hasn't seen action for years finds himself dealing with a group of terrorists.

It's his chance to be a hero.

Except, nothing is as it seems.

A short military conspiracy thriller that will keep you guessing.

Available at all major eBook retailers

False Flag

1991: A plan to destabilise Hong Kong is emerging; the key players are being put into place, the wheels are in motion and innocent people will die.

Frank Bowen is a Londoner on holiday in tropical Thailand. Half drunk and strapped for cash, he's the perfect bait for a political plot that will leave him running for his life, with nowhere to turn.

Available at all major eBook retailers
Paperback ISBN: 978-1-9997232-2-4

Pandora Red

Frank Bowen's mission is to find a GCHQ whistleblower but in doing so unwittingly risks everything, including his own family's safety.

As part of a covert team, assigned to dangerous missions, Bowen believes he knows what he's up against, until a team of Russian mercenaries are thrown into the mix, leaving everyone and everything hanging in the balance.

It's a race against the clock to save all that he holds dear and uncover the dark truths behind his mission.

Available at all major eBook retailers.
Paperback ISBN: 978-1-9997232-3-1

Blood Tide

Detective Douglas Brown transferred to Hong Kong to forget his past and the dark memory that still haunts him; Richard Blythe.

Blythe, an explosives expert gone rogue, had terrorised London and outwitted Brown, leading to the deaths of countless innocents.

Now the detective's worst fear has come true: Blythe free from prison to wreak havoc and lead Brown in a deadly cat and mouse game in the city of Hong Kong.

Available at all major eBook retailers.
Paperback ISBN: 978-1-9997232-6-2